The Box of Magic

Enid Blyton

The Box of Magic

THE HOCUS POCUS COLLECTION

Bounty
BOOKS

Published in 2014 by Bounty Books,
a division of Octopus Publishing Group Ltd,
Endeavour House,
189 Shaftesbury Avenue,
London WC2H 8JY
www.octopusbooks.co.uk

An Hachette UK Company
www.hachette.co.uk
Enid Blyton ® Text copyright © 2014 Hodder & Stoughton Ltd.
Illustrations copyright © 2014 Octopus Publishing Group Ltd.
Layout copyright © 2014 Octopus Publishing Group Ltd.

Illustrated by Martine Blaney, Maureen Bradley, Diana Catchpole,
Jane Pape-Ettridge, Andrew Geeson, Dorothy Hamilton, Georgina
Hargreaves, Ray Mutimer, Mike Taylor, Sara Voller, Janet Wickham,
Peter Wilks and Lynda Worrall.
Cover illustration by Lisa Evans.

ISBN: 978-0-75372-707-2

A CIP catalogue record for this book is available from the
British Library.

Printed and bound in Spain

CONTENTS

The Box of Magic

Once upon a time, when Muddle and Twink, the two brownies, were walking along over Bumblebee Common, they found a strange box lying on the path. Muddle picked it up and opened it.

"Twink!" he cried, in amazement. "Look! It's full of wishing-feathers!"

Twink looked and whistled in surprise. "Jumping buttons!" he said. "What a find! I say, Muddle, we'll have the time of our lives now, wishing all we want to! Come on – let's hurry home, shall we, and do a bit of wishing?"

Neither of the two naughty brownies thought that what they really ought to do was to find out who the box of wishing-feathers belonged to. No, they simply scurried to their cottage as fast as ever they could, Muddle carrying the box tightly under his arm.

They ran in at their little front door, and put the box on the table. They took off the lid and there lay the wishing-feathers, dozens of them. Do you know what a wishing-feather is like? It is pink at the bottom, green in the middle, and bright, shining silver at the tip – and it smells of cherry-pie, so you will always know one by that!

Well, there lay the pink, green and silver feathers, all smelling most deliciously of cherry-pie. Twink and Muddle gazed at them in delight. Twink picked up a feather.

"I wish for a fine, hot, treacle pudding!" he cried, waving his feather. It at once flew out of the window and in came a large dish with a steaming-hot treacle pudding on it. Unfortunately Muddle was in the way and it bumped into his head. The pudding fell off the dish and the hot treacle went down Muddle's neck. *Crash!* The dish broke on the floor.

"Ooh! Ah! Ooh!" wept Muddle.

"You silly creature!" cried Twink, in a rage, as he saw his beautiful pudding on the floor. "What do you want to get in the way for? Just like you, Muddle, always muddling everything!"

"You nasty, unkind thing!" said Muddle, fiercely. "Why didn't you tell me you were going to wish for a stupid pudding like this? Oooh! I wish the treacle was all down your neck instead of mine, that's what I wish!"

A wishing-feather flew from the box and out of the window as Muddle said this, and the treacle down his neck vanished – and appeared all round poor Twink's neck! How he yelled.

"I hate you!" he shouted to Muddle, trying to wipe away the treacle. "I wish you were a frog and had a duck after you!"

A wishing-feather flew out of the window once more – and, my goodness me, Muddle disappeared and in his place came a large green frog, who shouted angrily in Muddle's voice. Just behind him appeared a big white duck, saying "Quack, quack" in excitement as she saw the frog.

Then hoppity-hop went Muddle all round the room, trying to escape the duck. Twink laughed till the tears ran down his face and mixed with the treacle!

"Oh, you wicked rogue!" shouted froggy Muddle. "I wish you were a canary with a cat after you!"

Oh dear! Immediately poor Twink disappeared and in his place appeared a bright yellow canary, rather larger than an ordinary one. Just

10

behind came a big tabby cat saying "Mew, mew!" excitedly at the sight of the canary. Then what a to-do there was! Muddle, still a frog, was trying to escape the duck, and Twink, a canary, was trying to fly away from the pouncing cat. Neither of the two had any breath for wishes, and what

would have happened to them, goodness knows – if the cat hadn't suddenly seen the duck!

"Miaow!" it said and pounced after the waddling duck. With a quack of fright the white bird waddled out of the cottage, the cat after her. As soon as they went out of the door, they disappeared into smoke. It was most strange.

The frog and the canary looked at one another. They felt rather ashamed of themselves.

"I wish we were both our ordinary selves again," said Muddle, in rather a small voice. At once the frog and the canary disappeared and the two brownies stood looking at one another.

"This sort of thing won't do," said Twink. "We shall waste all the wishing-feathers if we do things like this, you know, Muddle."

"Well, let's wish for something sensible now," said Muddle. "What about wishing for a nice, big, friendly dog, Twink? We've always wanted a dog, you know. Now is our chance."

"All right," said Twink. "Let's wish for a black and white one, shall we?"

"No, I'd rather it was a brown and white one," said Muddle. "I like that kind best."

"Well, I prefer a black and white one," said Twink. "I wish for a black and white dog!"

Immediately a large black and white dog appeared, and wagged its tail at the brownies.

"I wish you to be brown and white!" said Muddle at once, scowling at his friend. The dog obligingly changed its colour from black to brown. Twink was furious. "I wish you to be black and white!" he yelled. The dog changed again, looking rather astonished.

"Now, don't let's be silly," said Muddle, trying to keep his temper. "I tell you, Twink, a dog is nicer if it is brown and white. I wish it to be—"

"Stop!" said Twink, fiercely. "It's my dog! I won't have you changing its colour like this! Wish for a dog of your own if you want to, but don't keep interfering with mine."

"I wish for a brown and white dog!" said Muddle at once. A large brown and white dog immediately walked in at the door, wagging its tail in a most friendly fashion. But as soon as the black and white one saw it, it began to growl very fiercely and showed its teeth.

"Grr!" it said.

"Grrr!" the other dog said back. The black and white dog then flew at the other and tried to bite it.

"Call off your horrid dog!" yelled Muddle to Twink. "It's biting mine! Oh! Oh! Look at it!"

"Well, you should have been content with one dog," said Twink. "You see, my dog thinks this is its home, and it won't let a strange dog come in. Quite right, too. It's a good dog!"

"It isn't, it isn't!" cried Muddle. "Oh dear, oh dear, do call off your dog, Twink. Look, it's biting the tail of mine."

"Of course it is," said Twink. "I tell you, mine is a very good, fierce dog. Tell your dog to go away, then it won't get hurt."

"Why should I?" shouted Muddle, in a temper again. "My dog has as much right as yours to be here. Isn't this my home as much as yours? Then my dog can live here if I say so! Oh look, look, your dog has bitten my dog's collar in half!"

Muddle was in such a rage that he ran to Twink's dog, his hand raised as if to smack it. The dog at once turned round, growled and tried to bite Muddle, who jumped away and ran round the room. The dog, thinking it was a game, ran after him, and Muddle was very much frightened.

16

"Call him off, call him off!" he yelled. But Twink sat down on the sofa and laughed till the tears ran down his long nose. He thought it was a funny sight to see Muddle being chased by his dog.

"I wish my dog would go and bite you, you horrid thing!" yelled Muddle. Then it was Twink's turn to jump up and run – for the brown and white dog ran at Twink, showing all its white teeth.

Twink ran out of the cottage followed by a snapping dog, and Muddle ran out too, the other dog trying to nip his leg.

"Oh!" cried Twink, as he was bitten on the hand.

"Oooh!" yelled Muddle, as he was nipped in the leg. "I wish the dogs weren't here any more! I wish we hadn't got those horrid wishing-feathers that seem to make things go all wrong!"

In an instant the two dogs vanished and the box of feathers sailed away through the air, back to the Green Wizard who had lost them that morning. The two brownies stood looking at one another, Twink holding his hand and Muddle holding his leg.

"The dogs have gone but they've left their bites behind them," groaned Muddle. "Why didn't you wish those away too, Twink? The feathers have gone now, so we can't do any more wishing."

"Well, our wishing didn't do us any good, did it?" said Twink. "Come on in, Muddle, and let us bathe our bites. We have behaved badly and we deserve our punishment. My goodness, if I find wishing-feathers again, I'll be more sensible. Won't you?"

"Rather!" said Muddle, limping indoors. But I don't expect they ever will find such a thing again do you?

The House
in the Fog

There was once a boy who didn't believe in fairies, or pixies, or giants, or dragons, or magic, or anything like that at all.

"But at least you know there were dragons," said Mary. "St George killed one. It's even in our history books at school, where it tells us why we have St George's cross on our flag."

"Believe what you like," said William, "I just don't think there ever were such things."

Now one day William had to go to a Cub meeting. He was a very good Cub indeed, and meant to be an even better Scout later on. He had his tea at home, then looked at the clock. "I must go, Mum," he said. "I've got to be at the meeting at six."

His mother peered out of the window. It was a dark evening – and, dear me, how foggy it seemed, too! "I wonder if you ought to go, William," she said. "It's getting foggy."

"Oh, Mum – what does that matter?" said William, putting on his Cub jersey. "I know my way blindfold! I can't *possibly* miss my way home."

Well, William was certainly a very sensible boy, so his mother let him go. He got to the meeting in good time – William was always punctual – and he had a very nice evening. Then it was time to go home.

The Cub-master looked out of the

door. "My word," he said, "the fog is very thick. I hope you will find your way home all right."

"Well, we all go the same way, except William," said John. "So we can keep together. What about William, though?"

"Pooh!" said William. "Do you suppose I'd lose my way in a fog! A Cub knows his way about even if he can't see a thing!"

And off he went out into the fog alone. Didn't he know his way perfectly well? Hadn't he walked the same road dozens of times? What did it matter if the fog was thick? He could *easily* find his way home.

But after he turned two corners he suddenly stopped. His torch hardly showed a beam at all in the thick fog. Was he on the right road? He must be! He couldn't possibly have taken the wrong turning.

He flashed his torch on the name of the road, printed on a wall nearby. Ah, yes – he was all right – it was Ash Tree Avenue. Thank goodness! He hadn't gone the wrong way after all.

"I've only to go down to the end of the road, turn sharply to the left, cross over, and then keep straight on until I get to my own house," said William to himself. So off he went again, his steps tap-tapping in the fog which now swirled thickly about him.

He went on and on. Wherever was the end of Ash Tree Avenue? Surely it wasn't as long as this! On and on and on. William stopped, puzzled. He ought to have come to the end of it by now, and have turned left.

He turned and went back. "I'll start at the top again, where the name of the

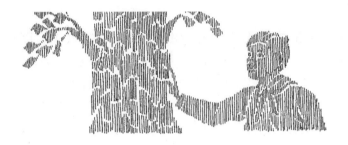

road is," he thought. His steps tap-tapped again as he went. On and on and on he walked.

He didn't come to the beginning of the road, where he had seen the name. Where was it? He had kept on the very same pavement and he hadn't crossed over at all. It *must* still be Ash Tree Avenue. But why didn't it end? He stopped again. He turned and went *down* the road this time. Surely he would come to the turning! On he went, but there really was no turning! What had happened?

"I'm not in a dream, I know that," said William. "I've just come from the Cub meeting, and I'm walking home in rather thick fog. And I'm on the right way. I'm not lost. I just can't seem to find the end of this road."

It was no use. He couldn't find it. No matter if he went up or down, there seemed no end and no beginning.

"This is absolutely silly," said William at last. "There's no sense in it. I shall go into one of those houses and ask my way."

He flashed the torch on the gate of the nearest house. He saw the name there, Munti House. He went up the little path and came to the front door. It had a peculiar knocker in the shape of a man's head. The head had pointed ears and a wide grin. William knocked on the door with it.

The door opened, and a dim light shone out from the hall. "Please," began William, "could you tell me . . ."

Then he stopped. Nobody was there. There was just the open door and the dark hall and nothing else. How peculiar! William peered inside.

A curious whistling noise came from the hall, like the wind makes in the chimney. "Well," said William, "if someone is whistling, someone is at home. I'll go in."

So in he went and the door shut softly behind him. He walked up the hall and came to a room without a door. Someone was whistling there. The whistling stopped. "Come in, come in," said a high little voice. "What do you want, William?"

William jumped. How did anyone in that house know his name? He looked round the room in surprise. A plump little man with pointed ears and remarkably green eyes was sitting in a rocking-chair by an enormous fire. Rockity-rock, he went, rockity-rock.

26

He looked at William and grinned.

"Why," said William, "you are exactly like the knocker on your door!"

"I know," said the little man. "Why shouldn't I be? Your name's William, isn't it? I'm Mr Munti, of Munti House."

"How do you know my name's William?" asked William.

"Well, I just took one look at you and I knew your name must be William," said Mr Munti, rocking furiously. "That's easy."

It didn't seem easy to William. He stared at Mr Munti, who stared back. "I came to ask if you could . . ." began William, but he was interrupted by a large black and white cat with eyes as green as Mr Munti's.

"MEEEE-ow," said the cat, walking into the room and patting Mr Munti on the knee. "MEEEE-ow!"

"Hungry, are you?" said Mr Munti. "Pour, jug, pour!"

There was a big milk-jug on the table and, on the floor below, a large

saucer. The jug solemnly tipped itself
and poured milk into the saucer below.

"Good, jug, good," said Mr Munti,
rocking away hard. "You didn't spill a
drop that time. You're getting better."

William stared in surprise. What a
peculiar jug! He looked at Mr Munti. "I
say," he said, "are you a conjuror?"

"No," said Mr Munti. "Are you?"

"No," said William. "I'm a little boy."

"Don't believe in them," said Mr
Munti, and he gave a sudden high

chuckle like a blackbird. "I never did believe in little boys."

William was astonished. "But you *must* believe in them," he said. "I've just been to a Cub meeting. I'm a Cub, and I—"

"There you are!" said Mr Munti grinning. "You're a cub. You're not a little boy. What sort of cub are you? I believe you're a fox-cub. You've got such a nice bushy tail."

William felt something swishing behind him and looked around. To his enormous astonishment he saw that a fine bushy tail hung down behind him. He turned around to see it properly – and the tail turned with him. He felt it – good gracious, it seemed to be growing on him, right through his trousers!

"MEEEE-ow," said the cat again and patted the little man on the knee.

"What! Still hungry?" said Mr Munti. "I never knew such a cat! There's a kipper in the cupboard for you."

The cat went to the cupboard door, stood on his hind legs and opened it. He sniffed inside the cupboard, put in his paw and pulled out a kipper. It landed on the floor.

"Shut the door, Greeny, shut it," ordered Mr Munti. The cat blinked at him with deep green eyes and carefully shut the cupboard door. Then he began to eat his kipper.

William stared, open-mouthed, forgetting his tail for the moment. What a clever cat!

"Well?" said Mr Munti, rocking away hard. "Did you say you were a fox-cub? Or perhaps you are a bear-cub? I see you have nice hairy paws."

William looked at his hands in horror. Whatever was the matter with him? He had big hairy paws now, instead of hands. He hid them in his pockets at once, full of dismay. What *was* happening? What was this little man with the bright green eyes?

"No – on the whole, I think you must

be a lion-cub," said Mr Munti, peering at him. "I never in my life have seen such wonderful whiskers. Magnificent. Aren't they, Greeny? Even better than yours."

"MEEEE-ow," said Greeny, and began washing himself very thoroughly.

William felt his face in alarm. Goodness gracious, there were long, strong whiskers growing from his cheeks – how very peculiar he must look! His paw brushed against his face, a furry, soft paddy-paw, just like a bear's.

"Please, sir," said William, beginning to feel scared, "I want to go home. I'm not a lion-cub, or a bear-cub, or a fox-cub – I'm a little boy Cub, a sort of Scout."

"I told you, I don't believe in little boys," said Mr Munti. "So I don't believe in your home either. I don't believe you want to go there because there isn't one, and I don't believe in *you*. Do you believe in me?"

"Well – what are you?" asked William, desperately.

"My mother was a pixie and my father was a brownie," said Mr Munti, rocking away.

"Then I don't believe in you," said poor William. "I don't believe in fairies, or pixies, or brownies, or dragons, or giants, or . . ."

"And I don't believe in little boys, so we're quits," said Mr Munti, with a wide grin.

"Ding-dong," said the clock loudly, and danced all the way down to the end of the mantelpiece and back again.

"Will you stop that?" said Mr Munti fiercely to the clock. "How often must I tell you that well-behaved clocks don't caper about like that?"

William began to feel bewildered. His tail waved about behind him. He could feel it quite well. His hairy paws were deep in his pockets. He could feel the whiskers on his cheeks. What was happening? He didn't believe in any of it, but it was happening all right

– and happening to him.

"I'm going out of this peculiar house," said William suddenly, and he turned to go.

"You might say goodbye," said Mr Munti, rocking tremendously hard and almost tipping over.

"Goodbye, Mr Munti," said William.

"MEEEE-ow," said the cat, and came with him to the front door. The cat stood up and opened the door politely. William went out into the darkness and the fog. The door shut. He shone his torch on the knocker head on the door, and then on the

name of the house on the front gate – Munti House. Who was Mr Munti really? Was he, *could* he be a conjuror? Conjurors did do peculiar things. But that cat, too – and the jug – and the clock!

"I shall certainly come back tomorrow and see Mr Munti again, in the daylight," said William to himself. He went down the road, hoping that he would find the end of it this time. And, to his great delight, he did. The fog began to clear a little, and he could see his way.

"Turn to the left – then over the crossing – and straight home!" said William, in delight. "Oh dear – what in the world will Mum say when I arrive home with a tail and furry paws and whiskers?"

She didn't say anything – because when William thankfully walked in his tail had gone, his hands were his own again, and there were no whiskers left. And what was more, his mother wouldn't believe a word of his tale!

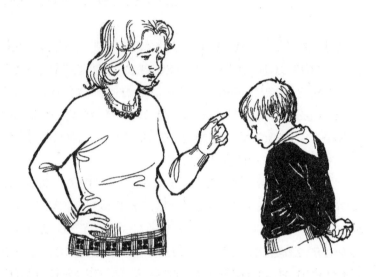

"Fancy you making up such a silly story!" she said. "You're very late, William – and you needn't tell me a lot of fairy-tales like that. Just tell the truth."

Now, the next day, as you can imagine, William went off to Ash Tree Avenue to look for Munti House, and the strange knocker on the door, and Mr Munti himself. And will you believe it, though he looked at every single house in the avenue at least three times, not one was called Munti House, and not one had a knocker in the shape of a grinning head.

Poor William was terribly puzzled. He told his story to several people, but nobody believed him at all. "How can you make up such a story when you've always said you don't believe in things like that?" said Mary.

He told it to me. That's how I know about it. "I've no tail left, of course," said William, "but see, there are a few little hairs still on my hands, and there's a place on my left cheek that feels a bit like a whisker growing. Do, do tell me what you think about it, please?"

Well, I don't know what to think! What do you think about it all?

Mother Dubbins
and Her Clever Duck

There was once a poor old woman who lived with Waddles, her duck, in a tiny cottage at the end of Hazel Village. She had very little money, hardly enough to live on. All her small savings were kept in a long red stocking and hidden behind the big clock on the mantelpiece.

One day Mother Dubbins came home from shopping and went to put a penny in the red stocking. But, dear oh dear! It wasn't there! Someone had stolen it.

The old woman was in a terrible way. She hunted here and she hunted there. She turned everything in her cottage upside down but it was of no use – she couldn't find the stocking in which were all her savings.

To make things worse it was the day

on which she had to pay her rent! What should she do when the landlord came? Would he give her time to pay, or would he turn her out?

The landlord was a horrid man. He was very unkind to old Mother Dubbins when he heard her tale.

"I don't believe you!" he said. "You bring me the money today, or I'll turn you out of your cottage and let someone else have it!"

Then he stamped off. Mother Dubbins knew quite well that she couldn't pay him any money, and at

first she could not think of what to do, for she was too proud to go and ask her friends for help. Indeed, they were almost as poor as she was.

She sat down and thought for a little while. Then she stood up and began to pack a few things in a bundle. She had made up her mind what to do.

"I shall go and seek my fortune," she said. "Lots of people do that. It is true that it is mostly young folk who go seeking fortunes, but I can think of no reason why I should not do so too. I shall go to the unkind landlord and tell him that he can sell my furniture, which will pay his rent."

So the brave old woman tied on her tall hat, put her bundle over her shoulder and went down the path to the front gate. In the garden was her duck. It was a fine, big bird, very plump and white, for Mother Dubbins loved it and took great care of it.

"Oh dear!" she said. "Who will look after Waddles the duck? Poor old Waddles, you must say goodbye to

your mistress, for she is going to seek her fortune."

Then the duck did a surprising thing. It quacked very loudly, and Mother Dubbins suddenly found that she could understand duck-language, though she never had before.

"Take me with you, old woman," said the duck. "I am fond of you, and would like to go with you. I may even help you, for I am wiser than you think. Also I can carry you on my back for I am big and you are small."

"Bless us all!" cried Mother Dubbins. "Now who would have thought that a duck could talk so sensibly? Well, Waddles, I will take you with me, and if you think you can carry me I shall be glad, for I am not used to walking."

"Get on my back now," said the duck, and she waddled over to Mother Dubbins. The old woman seated herself comfortably on the bird's soft back, and found that it was exactly right for her. She tied her bundle round the duck's neck, and then the two set off.

First she went to the landlord, and told him what she was going to do.

"You are a mean old man not to let me have time to pay you," she said. "But you can have my furniture, and that will pay the rent. I and my duck are now going to seek our fortunes."

"Ho ho!" laughed the landlord. "That is a funny joke! Ho ho!"

The duck looked at the scornful landlord and then suddenly jerked out her head. The man found himself pushed right off his feet, for the duck's powerful beak gave him a mighty blow in the waist. He went *splash*! into a

puddle, and sat there, very much
astonished. Everybody round laughed
heartily, for no one liked the landlord.

"Quack, quack, quack, right on his
back!" said the duck.

"This is a good beginning," said the
old woman. "I can see you are going to
look after me well, Waddles."

They set off again, and all day long
they travelled. Mother Dubbins didn't
get at all tired, for the duck's back was
very soft and comfortable. In fact she
almost fell asleep, but she wouldn't let
herself do that for she was afraid of
falling off.

After two days they came to a small
town. The old woman stayed at an inn,

and told everyone how clever her duck was.

"She has told me she will help me to make my fortune," said Mother Dubbins. "What do you think of that?"

"Can she cure deafness?" asked a man who was very deaf. "I should like to be able to hear, so perhaps your wonderful duck could cure me."

"Can you do that, Waddles?" asked Mother Dubbins, turning to the duck.

"Quack, quack, quack, quack, take a feather from my back," said the duck.

The old woman pulled a feather from her duck's back and touched the man's ears with it. At once he shouted in delight, and danced about gladly.

"I can hear, I can hear!" he cried. "I hear the birds singing, and the water-mill going round, I hear the children laughing, and the wind sighing! That is truly wonderful!"

But do you know, the ungrateful man wouldn't pay a penny piece to Mother Dubbins for giving him his hearing!

"No, no," he said. "You can't make me deaf again, and if you did, I wouldn't pay you!"

Then he ran off, chuckling.

"Quack, quack, quack, I'll get my own back!" said the duck.

"But how?" asked Mother Dubbins, dolefully. "We can't make him pay. We shall never make our fortunes at this rate, Waddles."

The duck went off by herself and visited the man's wife. The poor woman could not speak, and had never been able to since the time she was eight years old.

"Quack, quack, quack, quack, would you like your language back?" asked the duck.

The woman stared at the wonderful bird in surprise. Never had she heard a duck speak before, and at first she was too astonished to make any sign in reply.

Then she nodded her head.

Waddles pulled out a feather from her wing, and gave it to the woman. As soon as she touched it she began speaking, for her tongue was able to move again.

"I can speak, I can speak!" she cried. "Oh, how wonderful, dear duck! I will tell my husband when he comes home, and he will reward you!"

Just at that moment the man himself arrived home. He looked most surprised to hear his wife speaking, and he in his turn told her that he had got his hearing back.

"Give the duck a gold piece," said the woman. "She deserves it."

"Not I!" said the ungrateful man, and turned away, laughing. The duck said nothing more, but went waddling back to her mistress.

Now since the woman had got her

speech back, she felt that she must talk every minute of the day and night. Clack-clack-clack, went her tongue, and soon her husband became very tired of it.

"When I got my hearing back, it was not that I might listen to your tongue all day long!" he said angrily.

"Oh, you horrid, unkind man!" cried his wife, and she straightaway began to scold him hard. She followed him into the yard, and scolded him there. She ran after him down the street, and scolded him there, and she scolded him long after they were in bed and he wanted to sleep.

That was quite enough for the man. Next day he went to the inn where Mother Dubbins was staying, and begged her to get the duck to take away his wife's voice.

"Not I!" said Mother Dubbins. "You didn't pay me a penny for helping you, and you can't expect me to help you now."

"Quack, quack, quack, quack, would you like your deafness back?" asked the duck, suddenly.

"Oh, yes, anything to get away from my wife's tongue!" cried the man.

"You must pay two gold pieces then," said old Mother Dubbins.

The man sighed heavily, and took two gold pieces from his pocket.

"I have been foolish," he said. "If I had paid you one gold piece yesterday, I could have got my hearing back and never have heard my wife's voice, for you would not have given it to her. Now I must pay you two gold pieces to lose my hearing again! But as I shall certainly go mad if I hear my wife scolding me day and night, there is nothing else to be done!"

"Mean people always pay dearly in the end," said Mother Dubbins. She took another feather from the duck and touched the man's ears. Instantly he got his deafness back, and went to his home, glad that he could no longer hear his wife's scolding voice.

"This is the beginning of our fortune," said Mother Dubbins as she carefully put the two gold pieces away into her bag. "Now we shall be on our way again, Waddles."

They travelled on together until they came to a dark wood. Mother Dubbins was tired, so she slid off the duck's back and prepared to rest for the night.

Now near by there lived a great robber in a cave. He had much gold in bags, and was feared by all the country folk around. He was half a giant, and when he wished to rob anyone, he found it the easiest thing in the world.

He heard Mother Dubbins talking to her duck and came out to see who was near. When he saw the fine, fat duck he thought that here was a splendid supper for him!

"What are you doing here?" he roared at Mother Dubbins. "No one is allowed near my cave. You must go, old woman, and to punish you I shall take your duck and eat her for my supper!"

"Oh, please excuse me," said Mother Dubbins, getting up in a hurry. "I had no idea I was trespassing. Pray let us go on our way safely. As for the duck, she is no ordinary bird, and I could not let her be eaten!"

But the robber took no notice of her words. He simply picked up the duck and took her off to his cave. Mother Dubbins was frightened, but she

followed bravely, determined to rescue
her duck if she could.

"Quack, quack, quack, quack, do not
fear, I'll soon be back!" called the duck
as the robber took her off.

Soon the giant arrived at his cave,
and he made up a roaring fire, meaning
to cook the duck at once.

"You're the fattest bird ever I saw!"
said the robber, rubbing his hands over
the duck's soft back. "You'll make a
fine supper for me!"

But, dear me, when he tried to take
his great hands off the duck's back, he
couldn't! They were stuck there as fast
as if they had been glued!

"Quack, quack, quack, quack, put a
feather down his back!" called the

duck. At once Mother Dubbins ran in and took a feather from the duck. Then she stuck it down the robber's neck and waited to see what would happen next, for she knew that the feathers were full of magic.

Soon a curious thing happened to the giant-like robber. He suddenly began to grow small! In a short time he was no bigger than Mother Dubbins herself, and then he was even smaller.

"Stop, stop!" he cried. "What is happening to me? Are you a witch, old woman? Let me go back to my own size again!"

But he went on growing smaller and smaller, and then, when he was no bigger than a six-year-old child, Mother Dubbins pulled the feather out from his neck.

"You are too small to do any harm," she said. "You will never be able to rob people again! That is a good punishment for you!"

The old woman settled down in the comfortable cave and made the robber wait on her. He could not do anything but obey her, for all his giant-like strength was gone.

It was not long before the country folk missed the giant-robber and they came peeping around the cave to see where he was, for all of them hoped he had gone to some other place and would leave them alone.

They were amazed when they saw him! At first they could not believe their eyes when they saw the little dwarf-like man running about obeying Mother Dubbins.

"My clever duck did it," said Mother

Dubbins. "Perhaps you had all better come and see whether any of the things here belong to you. There is plenty of furniture in the cave, and I have found many bags of gold."

Soon all the people who had been robbed came to the cave, and they were very glad when they found their own belongings there.

"We will give you twenty pieces of gold for your good help," they said, and Mother Dubbins was delighted. She put the gold away in her bundle.

"We certainly are making our fortune!" she said to the duck.

Off they went again, and found many adventures up and down the countryside. The duck earned scores of gold pieces, and the old woman's bag began to be quite heavy.

Then one day there came a message from the king.

"His Majesty wishes to see your clever duck," said the messenger.

Mother Dubbins, very proud, mounted Waddles again, and made her

way to the city where the king lived.

She was taken to the throne room, and when the king saw her coming in with her great duck, he laughed.

"Welcome!" he said. "You are a strange couple, truly. I hear you are seeking your fortune, old woman."

"That is true," said Mother Dubbins, curtsying. "With the help of my good friend the duck, I am saving up many gold pieces."

"I want your help," said the king. "Can your duck find things that are lost or stolen?"

"Yes," said Mother Dubbins, and the duck answered too.

"Quack, quack, quack, quack, what you've lost I'll soon get back!" she said.

"Wonderful, wonderful," said the king, staring in admiration at the duck. "Well, I'll tell you all about it. Have you heard of the golden wishing-wand that a powerful fairy once gave to my great-great-grandfather, Mother Dubbins?"

"Oh, yes," said the old woman. "But surely, that is not lost, is it?"

"I fear it is stolen," said the king, sorrowfully. "I was holding a party a week ago, and I had twenty guests. I took out the magic wand to show them, and let them each handle it. Well, before it had gone halfway round the table, it had vanished, and no one knew where it was! What I want to find out is – who took the wand?"

"Quack, quack, quack, quack, don't you fret, I'll get it back," said the duck.

Then she and the old woman went out to make their plans. Soon Mother Dubbins went to the king again.

"Give another party, and ask exactly the same guests," said Mother Dubbins. "Say that you are giving it in honour of my clever duck. Tell everyone that they may stroke and pat her, for she will bring them good luck. But also say that if a thief pats her, it always makes my duck quack very loudly indeed. Then we shall see what we shall see."

The king did not know at all how this would find the thief for him, but he consented to do what Mother Dubbins advised. He sent out the invitations, and the guests all came, eager to see the wonderful duck.

Waddles had a beautiful blue bow tied round her neck, and stood in the middle of the king's hall. Everyone crowded round and admired her.

"Stroke her if you like," said the king. "She will bring you good luck. Only thieves and robbers must beware of touching her, for their hands always make her call out loudly."

So the duck had plenty of patting and stroking, but although the king waited patiently to hear if the duck cried out, she made no sound at all.

"Quack, quack, quack, quack, take your hands from off my back!" suddenly said the duck to everyone. So they all stopped patting her, and stood back in astonishment.

"Show me your hands," said Mother Dubbins, coming up to the guests. Everybody turned their hands palm upwards in surprise – and dear me, what a very peculiar thing – they were all as white as chalk!

Mother Dubbins looked at everyone's chalky hands, and then she suddenly came to a pair that were pink, and had no chalk on at all.

"Here is the man who stole your magic wand, Your Majesty," she said to the

58

puzzled king. At once two stalwart footmen took hold of the thief's collar, and held him tightly.

"What! Sir Oliver Sly!" cried the king. "Can it really be you who took my magic wand?" Then he turned to Mother Dubbins. "How do you know?" he said.

"Look at his hands," said the old woman. "His are the only pair not white with chalk. I filled my duck's back feathers with powdered chalk, for I knew that the only man who would not stroke her would be the thief, because he would not dare to in case Waddles quacked loudly at him! All the others patted her gladly, and unknowingly chalked their hands. Search Sir Sly's house, and you will find your wand!"

"What a clever duck!" cried the king. "Footmen, lock Sir Sly up in prison, and then send soldiers to search his house!"

The frightened courtier was hauled off, and his house was thoroughly searched. The magic wand was found locked away in a cupboard and was taken to the king, who was delighted to have it back again.

"Your fortune is made," he said to the old woman. "Here is a big bag of gold for you. Now return to your village, Mother Dubbins, and settle down there happily, for you have enough riches to last you for the rest of your life."

"Thank you, Your Majesty," said Mother Dubbins, gratefully. "I shall do as you say."

She and the duck went their way back to the village they had come from. Mother Dubbins was excited to think that she was going home again at last, and she wondered if anyone else had got her little cottage.

At last she arrived. Everyone came flocking out to greet her, for they had heard of her fame. Only the mean landlord did not come, for he was angry to think she had come back rich.

Mother Dubbins' cottage was empty, for no one would rent it from the unkind landlord after she had gone. As for her furniture, she did not bother about that, for she had plenty of money to buy more. Soon her little cottage was furnished, and very pretty it looked.

Then Mother Dubbins gave a grand party and invited everyone in the village to it. Even the horrid landlord got an invitation, but he didn't dare to accept it because he was afraid the duck would peck him again.

Mother Dubbins loved preparing for the party for she had never been rich enough to have one before. You should have seen the table when it was ready! It simply groaned with good things!

Mother Dubbins sat at the top of the table, and who do you suppose sat at the bottom? Yes, you are quite right – Waddles the duck! She wore a new pink ribbon and looked very grand indeed.

"Three cheers for the duck!" cried everyone. "Hip-hip-hip-hurrah!"

"Quack, quack, quack, quack, it's really lovely to be back!" said the duck, and beamed at everyone.

Billy-Dog

A big dog lived next door to the twins. He was black and brown and he had such a stump of a tail that it was hardly big enough to wag.

"He's a silly dog," said Jenny. "He really is. He doesn't know any tricks, and he won't ever run after a stick or a ball."

"He can't even sit up and beg when I show him a biscuit," said Johnny. "I've tried to make him, but he just falls over every time."

"And he still hasn't learned not to walk on the flower-beds," said Jenny. "He came in yesterday and walked all over ours. I think he's a stupid dog."

"He's old," said their mother. "He can't be bothered to learn tricks now. He should have been taught long ago not to walk on flower-beds, and to chase a ball – he'll never learn now. But he's a nice old fellow."

"He's dull," said Johnny. "He won't play, he won't run."

"The only thing he does is to go out looking for rabbits," said Jenny. "Granny told me. But she said he never, never catches one and she is sure that if a rabbit chased him, he would run away!"

Mother laughed. "Well, don't bother with old Billy-Dog if you think he's silly and won't play. I'm quite sure he doesn't want to bother himself with *you*!"

"We won't notice him at all," said Johnny. "He's just too silly for words."

So they didn't bother with Billy-Dog any more. They didn't call him to go with them when they went for a walk.

They didn't bounce a ball for him or throw him a stick. And Billy-Dog didn't take any notice of them either. He just lay in his front garden, or trotted off to look for rabbits in the woods, and didn't even wag his stump of a tail when the twins came by.

One day the twins went off to the woods to pick bluebells. Their mother had said she would like some because they smelled so lovely.

The woods were full of bluebells. They shone like blue pools between the trees, and there were so many that not even when the twins had picked a big bunch did the bluebells seem any less.

"We could pick a million and they wouldn't be missed!" said Jenny. "Oh Johnny, aren't they lovely? They look like patches of blue sky fallen down in the woods."

The twins wandered on and on. Johnny wanted to find a white bluebell because it was lucky, so they looked everywhere.

"It must be getting late," said Jenny, at last.

"I don't know the time, but my tummy tells me it's nearly lunch-time. I'm very, very hungry."

"Well, let's go home then," said Johnny, and he turned down a path. "Come on. I'm hungry too."

But they hadn't gone very far before Johnny stopped. "This isn't right," he said, in alarm. "I don't know this path!"

66

"Oh dear! We aren't lost, are we?" said Jenny. "I don't want to be lost." But they *were* lost! They went down this path and that path, but always they came to the end and found themselves even deeper in the wood. "These paths are just rabbit-paths!" said Johnny, at last. "They only lead to rabbit-holes."

"Johnny, shall we be like the Babes in the Wood and have to go to sleep and be covered up with leaves?" asked Jenny. "Oh, please find the right way."

But Johnny couldn't, and soon the twins stood under the big trees, with Jenny crying and Johnny looking very scared.

"Listen! There's a noise!" said Johnny, suddenly. They both listened.

"It's not a nice noise," said Jenny, tears falling down her cheeks. "It's a nasty snuffly noise. It sounds like a big animal. Let's hide."

But before they could hide, the big animal came round a bush, nose to the ground, snuffling loudly as he went.

And will you believe it, it was Billy-Dog! There he was, standing in front of the children, just as surprised to see them as they were to see him!

Jenny flung herself on him. "Billy-Dog! Oh, I'm so glad to see you! Are you lost too? Stay with us and guard us, Billy-Dog!"

Billy-Dog saw that Jenny was unhappy. He licked her face with his big tongue.

Johnny took hold of his collar. "Don't go away and leave us!" he said. "Let's all be lost together! Then when people come to look for you and for us, they'll find us all."

Billy-Dog pulled away from Johnny. He didn't like to be held by his collar. He got himself free and trotted away. Johnny ran after him. "Don't go, don't go!" he cried.

Billy-Dog stopped, but he trotted on again as soon as Johnny came up to him. Then when he was some way in front he stopped once more and looked round. His stump of a tail wagged itself.

The twins ran to him, but again he trotted away in front. He wouldn't let them catch him. It was most annoying.

"He's so *silly*!" said Jenny. "He just won't understand that we want him with us. I feel safe with him."

"He'll lead us deeper into the wood," said Johnny. "We'll get more lost than ever. But we'd better follow him, Jenny, because I feel safe when he's near, too."

So they followed Billy-Dog, and when they got left behind he stopped and waited for them. Then on he went again.

Right through the wood they went, and at last they came out into a field. Across the field went Billy-Dog, and under a gate. "Oh dear, wherever is he taking us now?" said Johnny. "We must be miles away from home!"

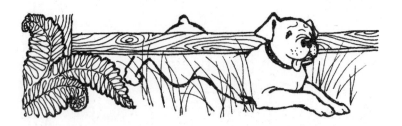

And then, when they had climbed over the gate into a lane, Jenny gave a shout.

"Johnny! JOHNNY! This is the lane that leads to our back garden! It is, it is! We're nearly home!"

So they were! They just had to run up the lane, and go into the gate at the end of their garden and race up to the house!

"You *are* late!" said Mother, meeting them at the door. "I was getting worried. I thought you were lost."

"We were," said Johnny. "But Billy-Dog was in the woods and he brought us all the way home. Fancy, Mummy, he knew the way quite well though we didn't. And he was very kind, he kept waiting for us to catch up with him."

"He's very clever," said Jenny. "Much cleverer than we are. *He* wasn't lost at all."

"Dear me, I thought you said he was silly," said Mother.

"We made a mistake," said Johnny. "We were the silly ones! Billy-Dog is old and wise. I shall take my pocket-money to the butcher this afternoon and buy him a juicy bone."

So the twins bought a big bone for Billy-Dog and took it to him. He was surprised and pleased. He wagged his stump of a tail and gave a little bark.

"He's saying thank you," said Johnny. "Billy-Dog, we think you're clever, not silly, after all. Please will you take us for a walk next time you go to the woods?"

"Woof," said Billy-Dog, just as if he understood. And do you know, the very next day when he wanted to go and look for rabbits, he went to fetch the twins, so that they could go with him!

"I think it's very nice of him!" said Jenny. I think it was, too, don't you?

The Train That Wouldn't Stop

In the nursery of the Princess Marigold was a toy train. It was a very fine one indeed. It was made of wood, painted all colours. It didn't run on lines; it trundled wherever it liked, round and round the nursery.

It was rather a magic train. In the cab of the red engine was a little knob. When Princess Marigold pressed the knob, the train began to run along, pulling the carriages behind in a long string. And it would go on running until the princess said the word "Hattikattikooli."

Then the train would stop suddenly and stand absolutely still until the knob in the engine's cab was once again pressed.

Marigold had great fun with the

train. She sat all her dolls and toys in it, pressed the knob, and off they went, trundling up and down. Sometimes she opened the door of her nursery and the train would rattle all down the passage and back, startling the king very much if he met it suddenly round a corner.

Now there were two small pixies who lived just outside the palace walls in a pansy bed. They were Higgle and Tops, and *how* they loved that little toy train. One day they climbed up the ivy, right up the wall and in at the princess's window, to see the train running.

They sat hidden behind a big doll on the windowsill, watching for the train to start.

Marigold put her rabbit into the cab of the engine to drive it. She put all the Noah's Ark animals into two of the carriages, her pink doll and teddy bear in the next one, and all the skittles in the rest. Higgle and Tops nearly fell off the windowsill trying to see what she did to start up the engine.

"She pressed a little knob!" whispered Higgle into Tops's ear, making him jump. "She did! That's how you start it!"

"I know. I saw," said Tops. "Oh, Higgle, if only the princess would go out of the room for a bit we could have a ride in that train!"

And will you believe it, somebody called Marigold at that moment, and she ran out of the room, closing the door behind her in case the train ran out.

In a moment Higgle and Tops were down on the floor, running across to the moving train. Higgle got hold of the rabbit. "Get out!" he cried. "You can't

drive for toffee! Let *me* drive!"

The rabbit pushed Higgle away. The pink doll began to shout. The bear tried to get out of his carriage to go to the rabbit's help. When Tops began to pull at the rabbit, too, he just had to fall off the engine. Then Higgle and Tops leaped into the cab and began to drive. Oh, how lovely!

They drove round and round the nursery at such a tremendous speed that three of the skittles fell out, and the kangaroo in one of the front carriages was frightened and jumped out in a hurry.

"Stop!" called the pink doll. "You'll smash us all up! Stop, I tell you!" But Higgle and Tops had never driven a

train before in their lives and weren't going to stop! No, they went faster and faster and faster. And when Marigold came back she was horrified to see her little train tearing by like a mad thing with all the toys hanging on for dear life and shouting in fright.

"Hattikattikooli!" she cried, and the train stopped so suddenly that everyone was shot into the air, and fell in a heap on the hearth-rug. The pixies shot out, too, and ran behind the doll's-house to hide. They were trembling with excitement.

"Bunny!" said Marigold, sternly, looking round for the indignant rabbit. "Bunny! Is *that* how you drive the train when I am out of the room? For shame!"

Behind the doll's-house there was a

little mousehole. Higgle nudged Tops. "Look! A mousehole! We'd better get down it before the toys come after us. They'll be dreadfully angry."

So down the mousehole they both crept. It was very small, and they had to crawl on their tummies – but, goodness me, it led right to the garden! That *was* a bit of luck for Higgle and Tops.

When the toys came to look for them behind the doll's-house, meaning to give them a really hard smacking for their naughtiness, they were not there.

"Just wait!" the rabbit shouted down the mousehole. "Just wait, you two! Next time you come we'll give you such a smacking!"

Higgle and Tops talked and talked about the train. How lovely it was to drive! If only it was theirs! What long journeys they could go on! What adventures they could have!

"Let's borrow it," said Higgle, at last. "Tops, we simply *must* drive it again. Let's go tonight and get it. We can creep up the mousehole. We know how to start it. Do let's."

"I'd love to," said Tops at once. "Oh, Higgle! Think of driving that train up hill and down dale, all across the countryside and everywhere!"

Well, that night the two of them went up the mousehole again, and into the nursery. The train was standing quietly in the corner. The toys were all at the other end, dancing to the musical-box. The rabbit was turning the handle, and nobody was looking round at all.

"Now's our chance!" whispered Higgle, and the two pixies made a rush for the train. They got into the cab, pressed the knob – and off they went!

The toys stopped dancing in fright and surprise.

The train rushed by them and out of

the open nursery door. Gracious! Where could it be going?

"It's those pixies! They've taken our train! How dare they!" cried the pink doll in a rage. But there was nothing to be done about it. The train was gone. It flew down the passage, bumped down a hundred stairs, ran to the garden door – and out it went into the garden!

"Here we go!" yelled Higgle, in delight. "Where to? We don't know and we don't care! Go on, train, go on, faster, faster, faster!"

All that night the train sped over fields and hills, through valleys and towns. When the dawn came, it turned to go back. Higgle and Tops had no idea at all where they were. They were just enjoying going faster and faster. The train hurried back over the hills and fields.

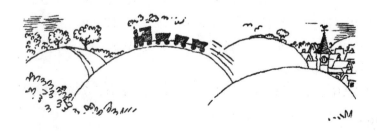

"I say – look!" said Higgle, suddenly. Tops looked – and there, not very far in front of them, were two red goblins, fighting hard. The pixies were very frightened indeed of goblins.

"Stop the train," said Higgle. "We don't want the goblins to see it. They'll take it for their own."

"I can't remember the word to stop it," said Tops. "You say it, Higgle."

But Higgle couldn't remember it either! Oh, dear! Now they would never be able to stop the train! It flew on towards the fighting, yelling goblins, and knocked them both flat on

their backs. The pixies just had time to
see an open sack filled with shining
jewels as they passed. Then the train
shot into a cave, bumping against the
wall, buried itself in the earth and
stopped with a shudder and a sigh. Its
wheels went round still, but the train
didn't move. It couldn't!

Higgle and Tops were thrown out.
They sat in the dark cave trembling.
They didn't dare to go out, in case the
goblins saw them.

Outside, the shouting still went on.
"You knocked me flat!" cried one goblin
to another. "Take that – and that – and
that!"

The second goblin howled. "Don't!
Don't! I'll go away now, really I will.
You can have everything yourself."

There was the sound of running footsteps. One of the goblins had gone. "Oho!" said the other. "He's gone. Well, I shall hide all the goods and keep guard over them. He may come back. I don't trust him!"

Higgle and Tops were sitting in the middle of the cave, still trembling, when something hit them hard. They jumped. Goodness, it was a glittering necklace! The goblin must have thrown it into the cave.

"A necklace!" whispered Higgle. "A real beauty! Where have they stolen it from?"

Blip! A ring hit Tops and another hit Higgle on the shoulder. Then came a shower of jewellery, falling all about the cave – *thud, blip, crash*! It soon looked like a treasure-cave, and Higgle and Tops didn't know where to go to avoid being hit as the goblin threw everything into the cave to hide it.

"My word!" whispered Tops at last. "I believe all this belongs to the queen herself, Princess Marigold's mother. Imagine it, Higgle! Those goblins must have broken in and stolen all this last night."

"Well – how are we to get it back to the palace?" asked Higgle. "Look outside there – the goblin is sitting at the entrance to this cave, guarding his treasure. We'll never get past him carrying all this. He'd catch us at once."

"We can't stay here for ever though," said Tops. "It's cold and uncomfortable – and I'm getting hungry. Think of something, Higgle. Use your brains!"

"Use yours!" said Higgle. So they sat and thought and the only noise in the cave was the sound of the train wheels still going round and round, though the train couldn't move.

"*I* know!" said Higgle at last. "Let's pull the train out of the earth it's buried in, and go out in that. We can pile the jewels in the carriages."

"And they'll all be jerked out, silly!" said Tops.

"I'll tell you what we'll do!" said Higgle, getting excited. "We'll wind all the necklaces and bracelets and chains round the wheels. They'll keep on then. And we'll drop the rings down the engine funnel. They'll stay in there all right. Come on, Tops!"

They set to work. They wound the shining necklaces and bracelets and chains round and round the wheels. Then they dropped all the rings down the funnel. The train looked very pretty indeed when they had finished with it.

"I guess a train was never dressed up like this before!" said Higgle, pleased. "Now come on, Tops – help me to pull it out of this earth. Steady on! Jump in as soon as we've got it free, because it will shoot out of the cave at top speed. It's still going, you know! We haven't thought of the word to stop the wheels turning yet!"

At last they got the engine out of the earth, and it stood upright. The wheels turned swiftly. Higgle and Tops jumped into the cab just as the train began to move. It went twice round the cave and then shot out of the entrance full speed ahead, its wheels glittering and gleaming in the morning sun.

How it shone with all its jewels! The goblin stared open-mouthed at this sudden, extraordinary appearance of

what looked to him like a glittering snake.

The train rushed over his legs and made him yell. Before he could grab it, it disappeared, shining brilliantly. The pixies laughed. "That was a fine idea of ours. We've escaped with all the jewels without being caught!"

The train didn't need to be told to go to the palace. It longed to be home! It shot off and soon came to the garden. It couldn't find any door open and raced up and down the paths like a mad thing. The king and queen saw it and stared in amazement as it ran by them.

"What is it? It's all shining and glittering," said the king. "It's as bright as those lovely jewels of yours that were stolen during the night, my love!"

Princess Marigold appeared. "Mother! Did you know my magic train was stolen? It's gone!"

At that moment the train shot back again up the path, shining brilliantly with the jewels round all its wheels. Marigold gave a squeal.

"Hattikattikooli! Hattikattikooli!"

Thankfully the train stopped just by her. She knelt down and looked at the wheels. "Mother! It's brought back all your stolen jewels! Do look!"

Higgle and Tops got out of the engine and bowed. "We brought them back to you," said Higgle grandly. "The two goblins stole them and hid them in a cave."

"Dear me – how very clever and brave of you," said the queen, pleased. "You shall have a reward. I will give you a sackful of gold all for yourselves."

"Thank you, Ma'am!" said the pixies, beaming. Now they would be rich. "We will take the train back to the nursery for you when you have taken all your jewels from the wheels and the funnel."

They ran it back to the nursery, feeling very pleased with themselves. The toys gazed at them in rage. Those pixies! They had taken the train all night!

"Good morning," said Higgle, stepping out. "We have an adventure to tell you. Listen!"

He told them all that had happened. The toys listened. "And," said Higgle at the end, "as a reward for bringing back the jewels, we are to get a sack of gold. Ha, a fine reward!"

"Have your reward if you like," said the rabbit, seizing the pixies in his strong

paws. "But let me tell you this – you're having a punishment, too, for taking our train. Why, you might never have brought it back. Six smacks each with the doll's hairbrush. Fetch it, Teddy."

Well, the pixies got their reward – but they also had their punishment, too, which was quite as it should be. They were so pleased to be rich that they gave a fine party to all the toys, and everybody went for a ride round the nursery, driven by the pixies.

They forgot the word that stopped the train, of course – but that didn't matter because all the toys knew it. They yelled it out loudly. Let me see – *what* was it? Dear me, I've forgotten. Do *you* remember?

Mister Wiggle's Scissors

Mister Wiggle was a tailor who made a lot of money. He lived in Fiddle-Town, and he owned a marvellous pair of scissors that people came miles to see.

These scissors were made of pure gold, and had a magic spell in them. Wiggle had only to put them down on a piece of cloth and say "Scissors, cut out a dress" or "Scissors, cut out a fine pair of trousers" and at once the golden scissors would set to work. They saved Mister Wiggle a lot of time and trouble besides giving him a great name for wonderful dress and tunic patterns.

Even the Queen of Fairyland had been known to order a special dress from him. But Wiggle wasn't at all vain. He lived in his little cottage and worked hard week in and week out.

There was just one thing he wanted and had never had – and that was a chance to be the chief brownie in Fiddle-Town and sit on the silver chair at all the town meetings.

But only clever brownies were allowed to do that, and although Wiggle was really a very thoughtful, wise brownie, he was so quiet that no one really thought of him as clever, and he was never voted for when a new chief brownie had to be chosen.

Now one day a strange piece of news went round Fiddle-Town. There was an empty house at the end of the village, and someone had taken it to live in and that someone was a witch! A witch in

Fiddle-Town! That really was a most extraordinary thing, for witches did not usually come to live near brownies. Brownies hated witches and feared them.

This witch was well known. Her name was Greeneye and you can guess why. She was a wicked, sly creature, always making up strange, cunning magic. She had been banished from the last town she had lived in, and when she heard of the empty house in Fiddle-Town she thought it would suit her well, and moved in the very next day.

"What are we going to do about Witch Greeneye?" asked the brownies at their next meeting. Mister Heyho, the chief brownie, sat in the silver chair and looked solemnly at everyone. Really, something would have to be done, he said. But nobody knew what!

"Well," said Heyho, rising from his silver chair, "if anyone thinks of a really good idea he had better be the next chief brownie, because I can't think of anything!"

Mister Wiggle the tailor went home

and thought hard. Here was a chance for him to be chief – if only he could think of a good idea. He sat down in his rocking-chair and thought for quite twenty minutes. And at the end of that time he smiled. He had thought of a plan.

His windows looked out on the back garden of the witch's house. Wiggle watched to see when the witch had her washing-day. On the next Tuesday he saw a great many clothes hanging out on the line.

He quickly put on his hat and went to call on the West Wind, who was a great friend of his.

"West Wind," he said, "will you do me a favour? There's a nasty old witch living just near my house and she has hung all her washing out on her line. Would you please go along and blow it all away and hide it for a little while where she can't find it?"

"But what for?" asked West Wind, in surprise.

"Never mind what for," answered Wiggle. "I've got a very good reason."

"Very well," said the wind, laughing. "It will be a good joke. I'll go along and do it now."

So when Greeneye the witch looked out of her kitchen window to see how her clothes were drying, she got a terrible shock – for West Wind had just that very minute blown along, and was sweeping every single one of her nicely washed clothes off the line.

Away they went, two dresses and two cloaks, three petticoats and a veil. West

Wind blew them up the hill and down the other side. Greeneye raced after them, but when she got to the top they were nowhere to be seen. West Wind had hidden them away very cunningly.

"Oh, you villain," cried Greeneye to the wind. "You've stolen away all my clothes! Now I shall have to go and buy some more!"

That was just what Mister Wiggle the tailor wanted. He peeped through his window and was delighted to see the witch walking towards his shop. Soon she had opened the door and walked in.

"Hello, Mister Wiggle," she called banging on the counter. "Where are you? Don't keep me waiting."

"Sorry," said Wiggle, coming out of his workshop. "I'm very busy, just at the moment!"

"Well, you may be busy, but you've got to put all your other work on one side and make me some dresses and a cloak," snapped the witch. "That

wretched West Wind has stolen all the clothes off my line, and I must have some more. I want them by tomorrow."

"I'm afraid that's impossible," said Wiggle, politely. "I've a tunic to finish for Heyho, the chief brownie, and a gown for Mrs Tiddlywinks, and a pair of trousers for her little boy."

"Don't be silly," said the witch, sharply. "You must put everything on one side and make what I want! You don't want me to turn you into a black beetle for disobeying me, do you?"

"No, I don't," said Wiggle, pretending to be frightened. "But I really must finish these jobs first, Witch Greeneye. But I have an idea – perhaps if I lent you my magic scissors you could get them to cut out what you want, and then sew the things together yourself. It's the cutting out that is so difficult, isn't it? But if you had my scissors, you could easily get them to do the hard part for you, and then it wouldn't cost you much to have the things you want – you could just sew up the seams yourself."

"That's a good idea," said the witch, who was always pleased to save money when she could. "Where are these scissors?"

"I'll go and get them," said Wiggle, and he went into his workshop, grinning to himself. He picked up his golden scissors, and took half the spell out of them before he gave them to the witch. She didn't wait to thank him but went straight off to her house with them, planning all the dresses she would have.

She pulled some material from a box and spread it out on the table. Then she popped the scissors on it and commanded them to set to work. In an instant they opened themselves and began to cut the cloth out in the shape of a dress. The witch was delighted.

She laid out another piece of cloth and the scissors cut out a cloak for her. Then she thought she would sew up the dress and the cloak, and she put the scissors on her kitchen dresser. But how great was her surprise to hear them still clipping merrily away! She looked up and saw

that they had jumped to the curtains
and were busily cutting them out in
the shape of a coat!

"You wicked things! Stop that at
once," cried the witch, in a rage. She
caught hold of the scissors, but let
them go with a shout for they quickly
pricked her hand with their points.
They flew to the tablecloth and began
to cut it up in the shape of a pair of
trousers. The witch was so angry that
she hardly knew what to do.

She did not dare to touch the scissors again, but she quickly looked up all her magic books to see what words she should use to make them stop. But she could find nothing at all to help her. It was dreadful.

The scissors cut up the carpet next and then all the cushions on the chairs. Then they neatly cut up the kettle-holder and flew into the bedroom to see what they could do to the bedspread and sheets!

The witch followed them, shouting and crying with rage, but it wasn't a bit of good. She simply could not stop those scissors! And, oh dear me, when they had finished cutting up everything they could, what do you think they did? They flew to the witch herself, and began to cut off her hair! Then they started to cut her clothes into rags, and poor Greeneye rushed out of the house in terror.

She ran to Mister Wiggle's and burst into his shop with the scissors busily cutting the laces of her boots.

"Mister Wiggle! What's wrong with these scissors? They won't stop cutting!

Put the right spell into them at once,
or I will turn you into an earwig."

"Well, if you turn me into an earwig,
those scissors will never leave you!" said
Wiggle, sewing busily at a coat. "Now,
Witch Greeneye, let us talk together. I
will tell you truthfully that I have taken
half the spell from my scissors – and I
don't mean to put it back again until
you promise me something."

"You wicked brownie! What do you
want me to promise you?"

"You must promise me to pack your
box and leave Fiddle-Town for ever,"
said Wiggle, sewing on a button at top

103

speed. "We don't like you. You're cunning and sly. We would much rather have your room than your company."

"Well, I shall stay!" shouted the witch in a terrible temper. "I shall stay – and I shall make all sorts of terrible spells to punish you and the other brownies!"

"Well, the scissors will stay too," said Wiggle. "Be careful they don't cut off your nose. I see they've cut off your hair already."

"Oh! Oh! Oh!" wailed the witch. "What shall I do? Go away, you hateful scissors! Stop cutting, I tell you!"

But the scissors took not the slightest notice, and managed to snip off the toes of both her boots.

Suddenly Greeneye boxed Mister Wiggle's ear hard and ran out of his shop, the scissors following her. She went weeping to her house and packed all her things into three big boxes. Then she clapped her hands seven times and four broomsticks came flying through the air. The witch tied a box on each of the three biggest, and then sat herself on the

smallest, with her big black cat behind her.

"Away! Away!" she cried. At once the broomsticks rose up into the air and Wiggle ran out to call all the brownies of Fiddle-Town to see the wonderful sight of Witch Greeneye really leaving the village at last.

"Hurrah! Hurrah!" they cried. "How did you make her go, Mister Wiggle?"

"Come here, scissors!" shouted Wiggle. He was afraid that his magic scissors might follow the witch in her travels. The scissors flew down into his hand and he shut them. They stayed still and cut no more until he next commanded them. He knew the magic word to halt them in their work.

Wiggle told all the brownies what he had done, and called West Wind to ask him where he had hidden the witch's clothes. The West Wind blew them out of a cave on the other side of the hill. Wiggle packed them into a basket and bade the wind blow them after the witch.

"We don't want anything belonging to

such a cunning creature left behind," he said. "Well, fellow brownies, I hope you approve of what I have done for you."

"Clever old Wiggle!" shouted everyone, and they hoisted him up on their shoulders. "You shall sit in the silver chair and be our chief brownie! Clever old Wiggle!"

Mister Wiggle was delighted. He sat down in the silver chair and beamed at everyone. It was the very proudest day of his life.

"Scissors, you must share my glory," he said, and he took them from his pocket and set them on the seat beside him. Then everyone cheered madly, and the scissors were so alarmed that they jumped back into their master's pocket again.

No one knows what became of Witch Greeneye. It is said that her broomstick bumped into a thunderbolt and disappeared. It is certain that she was never seen again!

Silly Simon and
the Goat

Simon had had a cold and his ears had ached. He had been very miserable. Now he was better and up again, but he was rather deaf. That was horrid.

"You'll be able to go to school again tomorrow," said his mother. "That will be nice for you. Today you can stay at home and help me."

So Simon helped his mother. He fetched in the washing from the line. He ran to the shop to get some butter, and he took the baby out for a little walk. He really was a great help.

"You have been quite a sensible boy for once," said his mother, pleased. Silly Simon wasn't always sensible. He sometimes did very silly things, and then his mother was cross.

He was pleased. "Well, you always

think I haven't got brains," he said. "But I have, Mum. I'm really a very clever boy."

"Well, I hope you go on being a clever boy for the rest of the day," said his mother. "Now, I'm going upstairs to do some things. Baby is fast asleep."

She went upstairs, and then she remembered that she wanted her old coat to mend. So she called down to Simon.

"Simon! Fetch me the old coat, will you?"

Simon didn't hear her very well. He thought his mother said, "Fetch me the old goat." He was rather surprised, but still, as he was feeling very good and obedient, he set off to fetch the old goat in from the field.

He caught the goat, and led him to the house on a rope. He called up to his mother. "I've got it for you."

"Well, bring it upstairs, and hang it over the banisters," called his mother. Simon felt more astonished than before. It was funny to want the old

goat brought into the house, but still
stranger to want it upstairs hung over
the banisters.

"The goat won't like it!" he called up
after a bit. But his mother only half-
heard what he said.

"Don't be silly!" she said. "It won't
hurt the coat. But hang it in the hall, if
you'd rather."

"Hang you in the hall?" said Simon to the surprised goat. "Which would you rather, goat? I can hang you in the hall, or take you upstairs and put you over the banisters."

The goat didn't seem to mind which. So Simon took it into the hall and looked at the pegs there. He tried to tie the rope to a peg, but the goat broke away at once, pulling the peg-rack down with a crash.

"Simon!" shouted his mother crossly. "What in the world are you doing? Be quiet."

"There!" said Simon to the goat. "You'll be getting into trouble if you make noises like that. You'd better come upstairs. I think it would be easier to put you over the banisters, after all."

So the goat was dragged upstairs. It made a great noise and Simon's mother called out again.

"You'll wake the baby! What are you making all that noise for?"

"I'm dragging the goat up," panted Simon. "It won't come."

"A coat isn't as heavy as all that," said

his mother, crossly. "What a fuss you make to be sure! I hope you're not dragging it on the floor."

Simon at last got the goat to the top of the stairs. He tried to get it across the banisters, but the goat simply wouldn't go. As fast as Simon lifted it up one end, it slipped to the ground the other end. It was a most annoying goat.

"Simon! Whatever are you doing out there?" called his mother. "Why can't you be quiet?"

"There!" said Simon to the goat fiercely. "You'll get me into trouble if you don't behave. Now, just you let me put you across the banisters!"

But it was no good. The goat wouldn't be at all helpful. It clattered with its four feet, it slid here and there, and was altogether most obstinate.

It suddenly got very tired of Simon. It backed a little way, put its head down, ran at Simon and caught him full on its head. It butted him hard, and Simon rose in the air with a yell, sailed down the stairs, and landed at the bottom with a

crash. He howled loudly. The baby woke up and yelled, too.

Simon's mother flung open the door to glare at Simon – but instead she found herself glaring at the old goat, who glared back, and looked as if he might butt her at any moment. Simon's mother hurriedly stepped back into the room and shut the door.

She called through it. "You bad boy, Simon! How dare you bring that old goat up here? Take him back to the field at once!"

"Well, you told me to bring him here and hang him over the banisters," wailed Simon. "You did, you did!"

"Oh! Oh, you foolish, silly, stupid boy!" cried his mother. "I told you to fetch my old coat – I wanted to mend it! Oh, why did I ever say you were good and sensible today?"

The goat trotted neatly downstairs and into the hall. It went into the kitchen and out of the back door. It had had enough of Simon and Simon's mother and the crying baby.

"It's gone!" said Simon. "But, oh, Mum, it's taken a rug with it to eat!"

"Oh, has it!" cried his mother, and shot out of the room and downstairs to catch the goat. But she was too late. The goat had eaten the rug.

Then Simon got sent up to his room, and he was very upset about it.

"I try to be good and sensible and

obedient and this is what I get for it!"
he wept. "I'll never try again."

"Well, if you do things like that when
you are trying to be good, you'd better
stop!" said his mother.

Poor Simon! You wouldn't think anyone would be so silly, would you?

The
Goblin's Dog

Once upon a time there lived a little boy called Willie. He had a dog named Tinker, and they often went for walks together.

Tinker was fond of Willie, but the little boy was not very kind to his dog. He was supposed to look after him and care for him, but many a time he went off to play and forgot all about him.

Tinker lived in a kennel out in the yard. It was a nice kennel, but it needed new straw each day. Sometimes Willie remembered, and sometimes he didn't.

Tinker liked fresh water to drink, but often Willie forgot all about refilling his water bowl. And once poor Tinker had no water at all because someone had upset it, and Willie hadn't noticed.

"Willie, it's cold weather now," his mother said to him one day. "Have you seen that Tinker has plenty of good warm straw in his kennel?"

"Yes, Mum," said Willie. But, you know, he hadn't – and Tinker had made his old straw so flat that there was no warmth in it at all. So he was cold at night when the frosts came. He thought of Willie in his warm bed, and how he longed to be able to curl up there with him. But he had to stay in his icy-cold kennel.

Now one night a small brownie came by on the way to the dairy to get a drink of milk. He heard Tinker shivering and popped his head into the kennel.

"What's the matter with you?" he said. "You seem very cold! Haven't you any warm straw?"

"Not much," said Tinker. "And my water is frozen too, so that I can't get a drink if I want to. Willie didn't take me for a run, either, so I haven't been able to get warm. Do you think you could bring me some water, brownie? There is some in the stream not far away."

"Certainly," said the brownie. He broke the ice in the bowl, emptied it out, and ran to the stream. He came back with some water and put it beside the kennel. "I wish I could get you some straw, too," he said. "But I don't know where there is any."

"Never mind," said Tinker gratefully. "Perhaps Willie will remember to get some tomorrow."

The brownie went to the dairy and had a drink of milk. He was unhappy because he couldn't forget the poor cold dog. He wished he could get some straw. He remembered that a wizard lived not far off, and he thought that maybe he would

120

know how to make straw out of magic.
So he went to his house and knocked.

A black cat opened the door and the
brownie went in. Soon he had told the
wizard all about Tinker. The wizard
listened, and he frowned deeply.

"That boy should be taught a
lesson," he said. He clapped his hands,
and the black cat appeared.

"Fetch the policeman," said the wizard.
The cat disappeared, and when it came
back, it brought with it a large policeman
with pink wings and a shiny face.

"Go and arrest Willie, who lives at the
Farm House," commanded the wizard.

121

"Bring him before the court tomorrow, charged with neglecting his dog."

The policeman saluted, flapped his pink wings and disappeared.

And soon, what a shock poor Willie got! He was sound asleep when he awoke to find a lantern shining on his face. The shiny-faced policeman was standing near by, and he spoke sternly to Willie.

"Come with me, little boy. I arrest you for neglecting your dog!"

Willie put on his coat and went with the policeman. The big policeman suddenly spread his wings and flew through the night, carrying Willie firmly

in his arms. There was no escape at all!

The little boy spent the night at the wizard's, and then the next morning the policeman took him to a big courthouse. Inside there was a judge who sat solemnly at a high bench, and had great wings like a butterfly's wings behind him. There were twelve pixies, brownies, and gnomes sitting at a table below, and there were six policemen, all with pink wings.

"This is Willie," said the policeman who had fetched the little boy. "He is here because of the following things: forgetting to give his dog fresh water – forgetting to give him straw for his kennel – forgetting to take him for a run – and altogether being very unkind."

"Very bad," said the judge, frowning at Willie. "Very bad indeed! Jurymen, what punishment shall we have?"

The twelve pixies, brownies, and gnomes who sat below the judge began to talk excitedly among themselves. Then a long-bearded gnome stood up.

"If you please, your worship," he said

123

to the judge. "We think he should be turned into a dog and sent to one of the goblins."

"Certainly, certainly," said the judge. "A very good idea!"

"But you can't do that!" cried poor Willie. "Why, my mother would wonder where I am!"

"Well, we will make your dog Tinker change into you," said the judge. "It will be a treat for him to have good food, plenty of fresh water to drink, and a warm bed at night. Now stand still, please, Willie!"

Willie stood still, wondering what was going to happen. The judge took up a wand that lay beside him, leaned over to Willie, and tapped him on the shoulder, saying, "A curious punishment you'll see! A boy you are – a dog you'll be!"

And then he said a very magic word – and my goodness me, Willie found that black hair was growing all over his body! His clothes disappeared. He grew a long tail. His ears became furry. His nose became long – he had paws

instead of his hands and feet. He was a
little black dog, and when he opened his
mouth to speak, he could only say
"Woof, woof, woof!"

"Take him to the goblin Workalot,"
commanded the judge. So Willie was
led out of the court on a chain, and
taken to a small cottage in a wood.
Here a little green goblin lived. He
didn't seem at all pleased to see Willie.

"I don't really want a dog," he said to the policeman who brought Willie. "Dogs are a nuisance. But if the judge says I'm to have him, I suppose I must."

There was no kennel for Willie so he hoped he would sleep on a nice warm rug in front of the kitchen fire. But a big grey cat suddenly appeared as soon as Willie sat down on the rug.

"Phizzz-ss-ss-ss!" she hissed at poor Willie. He ran back in fright, and got between the legs of the goblin who was just coming in with a bowl of water. Down went the goblin, and all the water splashed over Willie.

"Clumsy creature!" cried Workalot. He gave Willie a cuff on the head. Willie hoped he would get a towel and dry him, but he didn't. So the dog sat in a corner and shivered, for he did not dare to go near the fire when the cat was there.

Workalot was a very busy goblin. He ran here and there, he did this and that, and he grumbled and talked to himself all the time. The grey cat did nothing, but when Workalot needed help with a

126

spell, she walked up and sat solemnly in the middle of a big chalk circle.

Soon Willie began to feel very hungry indeed. The cat had a good dinner of fish and milk put down for her, but the goblin did not give Willie any dinner.

"I'll give you something later on!" he grumbled. But he quite forgot, so poor Willie had to go without. He thought he would whine so that Workalot would take notice of him. But as soon as he began yelping and whining, the goblin lost his temper. Willie put his tail down and ran under the table. But the goblin pulled him out, took him to the door, and put him outside.

It was pouring with rain. Willie looked round for shelter, but there was only one bush growing in the garden. He ran to that and crouched underneath, cold, wet and hungry. How dreadful it was to be a dog owned by an unkind master with no love in him!

The rain stopped. Willie crept out from the bush, but the door was shut and he could not get into the house. He looked at the house next door. A dog lived there too. But it was a dog that somebody loved, for it was well-brushed, cheerful, and not at all thin.

Willie wished he belonged to a good home too. How lovely it would be to be petted and well looked after!

The door opened and the goblin whistled. Willie ran in. The cat spat at him and Willie growled back. Workalot gave him a cuff. "Leave my cat alone!" he said. "Go into the corner and lie down."

Willie lay down. The cat sat in front of the warm fire and washed herself. There was an empty bowl not far from her, and Willie felt sure that it had been put down for him – with some meat and biscuits in, perhaps – and the cat had eaten it all up.

Willie fell asleep at last. But when night came, the goblin woke him up by fastening a chain to his collar and dragging him outside. He had put an old barrel there, on its side, and in the barrel he had put a handful of straw. "Get in!" said the goblin. "And mind you bark if the enemy comes!"

Poor Willie! He didn't know who the enemy was – and he was very frightened to think they might come!

He was cold too, for the wind blew right into his barrel, and he was so thirsty that he would have been glad to lick the snow, if there had been any. He began to whine dismally.

Out flew the goblin in a fine rage, and shouted at him.

After that, Willie didn't dare to make another sound. He just lay silent and hoped that the enemy wouldn't come.

Suddenly, at midnight, he heard a little scraping sound at the gate and he stiffened in fear. The enemy! The gate swung open – and in came, whoever do you think? Why, nobody else but Tinker the dog! He ran up to Willie's barrel and sniffed at him.

"I heard you were here, changed into a dog," he said. "They changed me into you – but I changed back at midnight and I've come to rescue you. You were never very kind to me, Willie, but I love you, and would do anything for you. Now keep still and I'll gnaw right through your collar."

Willie was full of gratitude to the little

dog. He kept still, and very soon Tinker's sharp teeth had bitten right through the leather. He was free!

"Come on!" whispered Tinker. "I know the way."

The two dogs sped through the night, and at last came to the Farm House. "Go to your room and get into your bed," said Tinker. "In the morning you will be yourself."

Willie pushed his way into the house and ran up the stairs. He jumped into his warm bed and was soon asleep. In the morning he was himself again.

"It's all very strange," thought Willie, as he dressed. "How kind Tinker was! How awful it is to be a dog belonging to an unkind master. I have been unkind to Tinker often. I never will be again!"

He ran down into the yard. Tinker was in his kennel. He wagged his tail. "Tinker! Tinker!" said Willie, putting his arms round the little dog. "Thank you for rescuing me! I'm sorry I was unkind to you. I will always love you now, and look after you properly!"

And so he did. Tinker has a warm kennel, plenty of fresh water each day, good food, a fine walk in the morning, and lots of pats. He is very happy – and I do hope your dog is, too!

In the Middle
of the Night

Harry was excited because he was
going to stay with his Uncle Peter and
Aunt Mary. He loved going to them,
because Uncle Peter was such fun. He
could play any game under the sun! He
loved football and cricket and tennis,
and he could run tremendously fast.
Harry often used to boast about his
uncle to the other boys at school.

"My Uncle Peter has a whole
cupboard full of silver cups he has won
for running and tennis and other
things," he said. "You should see them!
My Aunt Mary says it takes her two
days to clean them when they have to
be cleaned!"

"He'd better be careful a burglar
doesn't come and steal all those cups!"
laughed one of the boys. "Gosh, that

would be a fine haul for anyone."

"Pooh! No burglar could steal them," said Harry. "The cupboard is tightly locked, and Uncle has a big dog."

But all the same, a robber did come and steal those silver cups! It happened while Harry was staying with his uncle and aunt too, so it was all tremendously exciting, and very upsetting. Uncle Peter, Aunt Mary and Harry had all gone out for a walk one afternoon, and Sandy, the big dog, had gone too, so the house was left quite empty.

When they all came back – what a shock for them! Someone had opened the dining-room window, slipped inside and

gone to the cupboard where the silver cups were kept. A pane of glass had been neatly cut out of the front, and every single cup had been stolen! Not one was left!

"There must have been two men," said the policeman who was called in. "One to keep watch, and the other to do the job. I expect they had two sacks. It's a wonder they got away without anyone seeing them!"

It was a very strange thing, but not a single person had seen two men about – not even one man had been seen!

The two men who were painting the house, who had been working outside all afternoon, said that no one had been about at all. It was most puzzling.

Uncle Peter was terribly upset to lose all his beautiful cups that he was so proud of. "They will all be melted down into silver," he groaned. "And that will be the last of them!"

Harry was very sad too. He did wish he could help find the thieves. But though he prowled round and asked everyone if they had seen two men with sacks, or one man with a sack, he couldn't find out anything at all.

So, after a while, nobody did anything more about it, and the police said they were doing what they could but they doubted if the thieves would be caught now.

Harry begged his uncle to lock the doors of the house very well every night. He was so afraid that the thieves might come again and steal his new aeroplane, or even his penknife, which was a very fine one he had had for his birthday. So Uncle Peter locked up every door and window, and told Harry not to worry.

One night Harry woke with a jump. He sat up in bed. Something had awakened him – what could it be? It was the very middle of the night, and everywhere was dark. Was it a noise that had awakened him?

He listened – and then he heard a sound – but it was not the noise he expected!

It was a pitiful wail from somewhere

outside, and Harry's heart sank. He knew what it was – a rabbit in a trap in the field outside the garden. He had heard that noise before, and it made him very unhappy. The sound came again and again.

"Poor little bunny," said Harry. "It's little soft paw is caught. Oh, how I hate those traps! The poor little thing will be in pain all night long, and so terribly frightened."

He lay down – but the sound still went on, a dreadful wail like a baby crying in the dark. Harry couldn't bear it. He was a kind boy, fond of all animals, and he hated to know that anything was being hurt.

137

"I can't stand this," said Harry. "I'm going to get up and go out into the field. Perhaps I can find the poor little thing and rescue it."

He pulled on his jeans and his sweater and trainers. He groped about for his torch and found it in the cupboard. He slipped downstairs and out into the garden, switching on his torch to see the way he was going.

"Gosh, I hope there aren't any robbers about tonight!" thought Harry. "I shouldn't care to meet any! I forgot about them – oh, dear! Now I'm frightened!"

He stood in the garden in the dark, and wondered if he should go and call Uncle Peter. No, he might be cross. The rabbit wailed again and Harry forgot his fears.

"I'm not half so afraid as that poor little creature!" he said to himself. "I'm going on!"

Down the path he went, his torch throwing a beam of light in front of him. Slugs and worms slid everywhere, and a hedgehog hurried into the garden bed.

It was strange to be out in the middle of the night.

Harry came to the gate at the bottom of the garden. It led into the field. It was locked, so he climbed over it. He stood in the field grass and listened. The rabbit cried again, and Harry went towards the sound. The animal was frightened when it saw the beam of light, and lay still. Harry had to hunt for a long time before

he came across the trap, and saw the rabbit there, caught by its front paw.

Harry knew how to spring the trap. He had freed animals before, and it was only a matter of a moment or two before he had set the rabbit free. He looked at the frightened animal, and whistled in surprise.

It was a pure black rabbit! Harry had expected to see the usual sandy-coloured wild rabbit – but here was a lovely creature.

"You must be a tame rabbit, escaped and gone wild again," said Harry. "I've a good mind to take you home with me and bathe that paw of yours. Then I might be able to find your owner and take you back. You will be safer in a nice hutch than running about the field."

The rabbit was very tame. It stayed by Harry and let him stroke it. He lifted it up and walked back over the field with the rabbit. It was awkward climbing over the gate, but he managed it. He got back home and took the rabbit into the bathroom.

He gently bathed the hurt paw. Then he bound it up. The rabbit let him do everything without a murmur, and seemed delighted to have a friend like Harry.

"Now I wonder what I should do with you?" said the little boy. "I know! I can put you in the box downstairs in the kitchen, the one Puss-Cat had for her kittens."

So the rabbit slept there for the night, with a board over the top of the box so that he could not jump out and use his hurt paw.

Uncle Peter and Aunt Mary were most astonished when they heard about the rabbit and how Harry had gone to get him in the middle of the night.

"You deserve a silver cup for that!" said Uncle Peter. "Weren't you afraid, Harry?"

"Yes, I was rather," said Harry, blushing red. "But I thought the rabbit must be more afraid than I was!"

Uncle Peter made a nice hutch for the rabbit, and he went to live there while

his paw was getting better. Aunt Mary asked everyone she knew if they had lost a fine black rabbit, but nobody had.

"Perhaps I will be able to keep him for my own," said Harry. "He is such a dear, and so gentle and tame. He doesn't even run away when I put him on the lawn, Auntie."

"Well, let him loose sometimes, if you are there to watch him," said Uncle Peter. "But don't let him eat my lettuces, will you?"

Soon the black rabbit was so tame that Harry let him out every day in the garden. His paw was healed, and he was very happy. Harry played with him each day and hoped that he wouldn't hear of anyone who had lost the rabbit. He did so want to keep him for his own.

And then one morning the rabbit disappeared! Harry had gone indoors to get a book, and had left him eating the grass on the lawn – and when he came back there was no rabbit to be seen!

Harry called him, "Bunny, Bunny, Bunny!"

But no rabbit came. Then the little boy began to look for him – and he soon found him! He had gone down to the bottom of the garden and was busy digging a burrow under the hedge there! Harry watched him. He saw how he scraped out the earth with his front paws and shot it out behind him with his back ones. When he thought the rabbit had done enough digging he picked him up and carried him back to the hutch.

Then he went to look at the tunnel the rabbit had made. He bent down and put his arm into it to see how far the rabbit had gone – and he felt something down there!

Harry took hold of it and pulled. It felt like a bit of sacking – and as he pulled, the boy heard a clinking sound. And at once a thought rushed into his head.

"I believe there's a sack buried here – with Uncle's cups in it!" he thought. "Oh, I wonder if it is!"

He pulled and tugged, and sure enough

he was right. A big sack was buried there – and Peter saw at once that it was full of the stolen silver cups. The little boy stood and thought for a moment, and then he fetched a spade. Instead of digging up the sack, he put it back and filled the hole neatly to make it all seem as if no one had been there at all. Then he hurried in to tell Uncle Peter.

His uncle and aunt were most astonished.

"And, Uncle Peter!" said Harry, in excitement. "I've covered up the hole – and I thought if you hid in the shed nearby at night, you could see who comes to get the sack – and then you will know who the thief is!"

"I've a very good idea who the thief is now," said Uncle Peter sternly. "I think it's the painters. But it's a good idea of yours, Harry, to hide in the shed and catch the thieves red-handed. I'll ring up the police and tell them. I shouldn't be surprised if they fetch the sack tonight, because they are finishing the job tomorrow – and no doubt mean to take the cups with them!"

The police were most interested in Uncle Peter's news – and two police-men were sent down that night to hide in the shed with Uncle Peter. Harry begged to be allowed to hide too.

"Oh, please do let me!" he cried. "It was my discovery. Do let me share in the excitement."

"Very well," said Uncle Peter. "You may. But you're to keep inside the shed all the time – you're not to come out at all, even when we go out and catch the thief."

So Harry promised, and that night he and Uncle Peter and the policemen all crept down silently to the shed. They slipped inside and sat down on some sacks to wait. There was a moon that night so it would be easy to spy the thief if he did come. The hedge was well lit by the moon, and Harry knew exactly where the sack was hidden.

In the middle of the night there came the sound of soft footsteps down the

garden path. Someone was coming! Harry was so excited as he and the others peered out of the small window of the shed. They had cleaned it so that they might see clearly through it.

"It's Jones, the painter!" whispered Uncle Peter to the policemen. "Just what I thought! And listen – here's someone else!"

Another figure came quietly up and spoke in a low voice. It was the man who worked with him! So there had been two thieves after all! The police had been right.

The two began to dig. Soon they came to the sack and pulled it out. The painter threw it over his shoulder and the cups made a jangling sound.

"Now!" said one of the policemen. The door of the shed was flung open and out rushed Uncle Peter and the policemen. Harry had to stay behind as he had promised, but he did wish he could go and help too. But there was no need for his help. Jones, the painter, dropped the sack in dismay, and at the same moment one policeman clicked the handcuffs round his wrists.

His accomplice was caught by the other policeman. "He made me help him!" said the man.

"You can tell me all about that later," said the policeman sternly. Then the two were marched off to the police car, and Harry was told to go to bed.

All Uncle Peter's cups were put back in the cupboard, after Aunt Mary and Harry had spent two whole days in cleaning them. They were very stained and dirty from their stay in the damp sack. Uncle Peter was delighted to see them back, and he stood a long time looking at them shining brightly in their glass-fronted cupboard. Then he turned to Harry.

"Well, Harry," he said, "it's all because of you that I got back these cups of mine! If you hadn't been brave that night and gone to get that poor rabbit – and if he hadn't dug in the garden and found that sack – I'd have lost my cups for good! I shall give you another black rabbit to match yours, Harry, and a new hutch. You can take them home when you go, and I know they will be happy with you!"

Wasn't that nice of Uncle Peter? Harry was delighted! He has a fine new hutch now, and two fat and glossy black rabbits – and seven small baby rabbits besides! Isn't he lucky?

But he deserves his luck, because he was kind and brave, the sort of boy that anyone would be pleased to have for a friend!

The Rub-Away
Flannel

Meanie, the goblin, didn't like anyone.
Nobody liked him, either. He was just
like his name!

"He's mean to his poor old dog," said
the balloon-woman. "He never gives
him enough straw in his kennel, and
half-starves him."

"And his hens are as skinny as he is,"
said the paper-man. "So is his cat. He's
a regular meanie!"

Nobody asked him to their parties.
Nobody offered him fruit from their
garden. He only worked for old Mrs
Crosspatch – and that was because
nobody else would have him!

Old Mrs Crosspatch was half a witch.
You could tell that by her green eyes.
She didn't make spells or magic
nowadays, though, because she had

forgotten them all. Meanie wished he knew some of the magic she had known. Ah – he would put a few spells on some of the people he knew, then!

Now, one day, when Meanie was turning out an old chest for Mrs Crosspatch, he came across a square of white flannel. "What's this, Mrs Crosspatch?" he asked.

She looked at it. "I've forgotten what I used it for," she said. "Throw it away. There might be a spell of some kind in

it, so be careful. Has it got letters in one corner?"

"Yes," said Meanie. "But so faint that I can't read them."

"Ah, well – burn the thing," said Mrs Crosspatch. "It's no use now."

Meanie put it aside to burn. But something happened before he took it to the bonfire. He saw a dirty spot on the table, and took up the flannel cloth and rubbed the spot.

And, goodness me, a hole appeared in

the table. A hole! Right *through* the table, too. Meanie stared in horror. What had he done? He looked at the bit of flannel in his hands.

He rubbed the table again in another place – and another hole appeared. Then Meanie grinned slyly. He knew what magic had been in this flannel – it had once been a Rub-away Cloth! Whatever was rubbed with it disappeared.

Meanie was overjoyed. Fancy having a Rub-away Cloth that still worked! Why, no one had heard of one for years and years. He wasn't going to burn it – he was going to keep it and use it.

He would rub away the new wall that Mr High-Hat had built round his garden. That would serve him right for not giving Meanie any apples from his trees.

He would rub away Dame Ribby's gate. That would punish her for scolding him about his half-starved dog. He would rub away all the clothes on Mother Smiley's line. She would be sorry then for telling him he ought to wash his neck.

What a lot of things he would do! He would rub a hole in Mr Winky's henhouse, and all his hens would escape. He would – he would – well, there was really no end to the mean things he could do.

He did one or two on the way home. He rubbed the knocker off Mrs Minny's front door. He rubbed away the top of Miss Millikin's hedge. How funny it looked! He rubbed away the tail of a cat who was sitting on a wall. He got scratched for that, but he didn't mind.

He went home, grinning to himself. What a wonderful thing, to have a Rub-away Cloth that nobody knew anything about. Why, he would soon be the most powerful man in the village!

"I won't stand any nonsense from anyone!" he said, as he got himself a meal. "If the chief of the village comes to scold me, I'll rub his head over with my flannel – and there he'll be, without a head. If anyone comes to beat me, I'll rub the stick away – and his hands, too, if he isn't careful."

He ate his supper, thinking of all the
things he would do. His cat reached out
a paw and caught hold of the magic
flannel. It rubbed on the edge of the
table – and there was Meanie's table,
without an edge on one side!

He was cross. He snatched up the
cloth and tried to rub out his cat – but
she was too quick for him and leapt out
of the window. She didn't trust Meanie!

"I'd better take my cloth with me
wherever I go in case the cat gets hold of
it," thought Meanie, and he picked it
up. He went into the bathroom and shut
the door so that the cat wouldn't get in.
"I'm very dirty," he said. "I'll have a
bath. Then I'll dress up in my best and

go out and do a bit of rub-away magic in the village! I'll make everyone stare!"

He turned on the water. He undressed. He got into the bath and lay there, enjoying the warmth. Then he sat up and found the soap. He soaped himself well, and began to feel cleaner than he had felt for a long while.

"Now for my flannel," he said, and reached out for it. But – yes, you've guessed right – he took up the magic flannel instead! It was really very like

his own. And he rubbed himself all over with it, back and front. He didn't notice what was happening until he was almost finished.

He wasn't there! He had rubbed himself out. Not a bit of him could be seen – except the toes of his feet. He hadn't rubbed those with his flannel.

Well, that was the end of Meanie, of course. Nobody ever knew what had happened to him, and only the cat saw some toes tapping about the garden one day, all by themselves.

Mrs Crosspatch guessed a little, when she heard that a knocker had been rubbed away, and saw the top of Miss Millikin's hedge. "That must have been my old Rub-away Cloth Meanie took," she said to herself. "And somehow or other he's rubbed himself out. Well, it serves him right. Nobody will miss old Meanie."

I've often wondered what happened to the cloth.

Who took it out of the bath, and where did it go? Maybe it will still turn up somewhere. You never know.

The Cross Shepherd

Dick wheeled his car out of the shed and got into the driving seat. It was a very nice little car, bright red with silver wheels, and he was very proud of it. It had room for him at the front, and for one more rather small passenger.

The car had a hooter, and two lights in front that you could switch on. Dick worked it with pedals, and could get along very fast indeed. He raced off down the lane at top speed.

"I'm going to see the lambs jumping about in the field!" he called to his mother. "I'll be back in good time for lunch."

He was soon at the big field where the lambs played around the mother sheep. Dick loved to watch them, for they were really very funny. They sometimes jumped on to the top of their mothers – then the big sheep got angry and shook them off.

Dick left his car outside the gate and climbed over into the field. The lambs knew him and came running up. Dick picked one up and cuddled it.

Then a cross voice suddenly came over the field and made Dick jump.

"Put that lamb down! And get out of the field!"

Dick put the lamb down quickly. He looked to see who was shouting, and he saw a bent old shepherd standing at the door of his hut on the other side of the field. The shepherd was waving his stick at Dick as if he meant to hit him with it.

"I wasn't hurting the lamb!" called Dick. "I was only hugging it!"

"You might drop it and break its leg!" shouted back the cross shepherd. "I haven't sat up all night long in the cold winter with my lambs just to let a tiresome boy frighten them and hurt them! You get out of the field – you'll be leaving the gate open next, and letting all the sheep into the road. Be off with you!"

"I couldn't leave the gate open because I always climb over it!" shouted back Dick.

"Now don't you stand there talking to me like that!" said the old shepherd, and he took two or three steps across the field. Dick was really afraid of him, and he ran to the gate, climbed over it,

163

and was soon in his car. He pedalled off down the lane to the hills, thinking that the old shepherd was a very horrid man.

He drove his little car quite a long way, following the paths that ran over the hills. Then he began to feel hungry, so he knew it was time for his lunch.

He pedalled back. It was mostly downhill, so he was soon able to take his feet off the hurrying pedals and put them on the little ledges inside the car, pretending that he really was driving it, just as his father drove the big car.

He came to a little bridge over a stream and stopped for a moment to get out of the car and lean over the side of the bridge to see if there were any fish in the water.

There were no fish – but there was something else! There was a little lamb, struggling to get out of the stream!

"There's a lamb fallen into the water!" said Dick, in surprise. "The banks are so steep just here – it must have been a horrid fall. Poor little thing! Whatever can I do to help it?"

Dick ran down to the side of the stream. He looked at the water, which was fairly deep. He could see that the lamb would soon drown if he did not get it out. But the banks of the stream were so steep that it would be very difficult indeed to reach the lamb.

Dick thought for a moment. No – there was absolutely nothing else to do but to jump right into the water, lift up the lamb, and then try to climb out again. He would get very wet but it couldn't be helped.

So into the water he jumped. *Splash!* It was nearly up to his waist! The lamb was caught against an old branch that had fallen into the water and become fixed against the bridge. Dick waded to it.

He lifted the lamb up gently and put it round his neck as he had seen the shepherd do when he wanted to carry a lamb and yet keep his hands free. Then he turned to climb out of the stream. It was very difficult.

He lifted the lamb off his shoulders first and laid it down on the bank. Then he tried to scramble up the steep slope. At last he managed to climb up, and he bent over the lamb.

It could not walk. Dick saw that something had hurt its two front legs. Perhaps they were broken. The lamb lay there looking up at him out of frightened eyes.

"You are begging me for mercy," said Dick, "but you needn't. I only want to help you!"

He put the lamb over his shoulder again, meaning to carry it all the way back to the farm and come back for his car later. But the lamb was well grown and very heavy. Dick knew he couldn't possibly carry it very far. It couldn't walk – so what was he to do?

"I know!" he said suddenly, to the surprised lamb. "You shall be the passenger in my car! I can drive you back easily then."

He put the lamb carefully on the seat next to the wheel. Then he climbed into the driving seat and took hold of the wheel. His wet feet found the pedals and off he went. The lamb lay beside him, feeling more and more surprised, but it trusted this boy with the gentle hands, and was no longer quite so afraid.

People were most astonished to see a lamb as a passenger in Dick's little car! They turned and stared in amazement.

"Did you see that?" they said to one another. "That boy had a lamb in his car!"

"Oh dear!" said Dick to himself, as he pedalled along. "I've got to go and see that cross old shepherd now. I can't just put the lamb into the field and hope he will see it, because he mightn't notice it was hurt, and it does need its legs mended. But surely he would notice by the evening! Shall I just put the lamb through a hole in the hedge and leave it there without saying anything?"

Dick looked at the lamb. It looked back at him. It had a little black nose and wide-staring eyes. Dick liked it very much, and he suddenly knew quite

certainly that he couldn't push the
little creature through the hedge and
leave it. He must take it to the
shepherd, even though he might be
shouted at.

He stopped his car outside the gate.
He took the lamb in his arms, opened
the gate, shut it behind him, and
walked over the field towards the
shepherd's hut. The sheep set up a
great baaing when they saw him, and
the old shepherd at once appeared at

the door of his hut. When he saw Dick carrying one of the lambs again, he went red with rage.

"Didn't I tell you to leave my lambs alone!" he yelled. "Didn't I tell you to get out of my field! You wait till I catch you, you tiresome boy!"

But Dick didn't run away. He went on towards the shepherd, his heart beating fast. The shepherd raised his stick as if he was going to beat Dick, but the boy called to him.

"Wait! Wait! This lamb of yours is hurt! I found it in the stream, and its legs are hurt. It must have slipped out of the field and run away."

The shepherd at once took the lamb from Dick. He looked at its legs. "They're broken," he said.

"Can you mend them?" asked Dick anxiously.

"They'll mend themselves if I see to them now," said the shepherd. "You can help me if you like."

"Oh, thank you," said Dick. He followed the shepherd into the hut, and

together the two of them gently bound up the little hurt legs. The shepherd made clever wooden splints that he bound fast to each leg. The lamb did not make a sound, but lay quite still, looking up at the two who were caring for it.

"You're wet," said the shepherd to Dick.

"Yes. I had to jump in the stream to get the lamb," said Dick.

"This lamb is heavy," said the shepherd. "Surely you didn't carry it all the way here from the stream?"

"No. I couldn't," said Dick. "I brought it along in my little car. It was my passenger! But I was afraid of bringing the lamb to you because you shouted at me this morning and were very cross."

"Ah! I didn't know then what sort of a boy you were," said the old shepherd. "I get boys in here that break down my hedges and frighten my sheep. So I turn them out of my field. But you can come every day, if you like, and you and I will sit here and watch the lambs playing. I can tell you many a strange tale about lambs and sheep."

"Oh, thank you," said Dick. "Now I must go home to my lunch. I'll come again tomorrow."

"You come and have lunch with me tomorrow," said the old shepherd. "I'll get my wife to make us a picnic lunch, and we'll talk together. I could do with

172

a boy like you for company sometimes!"

Dick went home proudly. The cross shepherd wanted him for a friend! No other boy had ever been able to make friends with the old chap – but Dick could go and have lunch with him the next day.

Now the two are fast friends – and the lamb is quite better. It frisks up to meet Dick when ever it sees the boy coming along in his car – and do you know, it lets him take it for a ride once a week down to the village. It sits beside Dick, just like a proper passenger.

You should see how every one stares!

The
Biscuit Tree

Once there was a brownie called Mickle who was very poor. He lived in a tumbledown cottage, and grew potatoes and cabbages in his garden, and nothing else, because it was so small.

But though he was poor he was as kind as could be. If anyone came knocking at his yellow front door begging for a penny, he would shake his head and say, "I haven't even a ha'penny. But you may have a slice of bread, or two or three potatoes."

If anyone wanted help, Mickle would always run to give it. When old Dame Fanny broke her leg, he went in to sweep and dust her cottage every day, and he fed her hens so well that they laid even more eggs than usual.

And when Mr Winkle had his roof blown off in a storm, Mickle took a ladder, and spent the whole day mending Winkle's roof most beautifully.

Most people knew how to reward Mickle for his kindness. They would give him a few biscuits.

Mickle was so poor that he never bought a biscuit for himself. His meals were mostly bread, potato, and cabbage, sometimes with soup for a treat.

And he did love biscuits so much!

"I really don't know which biscuits I love most," he would say. "The gingersnaps are marvellous – such a lovely taste. And the chocolate biscuits that Dame Fanny makes simply melt in my mouth. And as for those little biscuits with the jam in the middle, well, I could eat them all day long!"

Now one day Mickle had a bit of bad luck. A goat got into his garden and ate all his winter cabbages! And when he went to his sack of potatoes to help himself to one or two, he found that a rat must have told his family about them, for nearly all had disappeared through a hole at one end of the sack!

Mickle could have cried! All his winter greens gone – and most of his potatoes! What was he to live on now?

He went indoors. He had been to help Pixie Lightfoot to dig her garden that day, and she had given him six pat-a-cake biscuits as a reward. He had meant to keep them for Sundays, and eat one each Sunday for six weeks at teatime. But today he was so hungry that he felt he could eat them all!

Now just outside at that very moment was a little beggar-child. Her father was a tramp who was walking through the village. She was ragged and cold, and when she saw the smoke rising from Mickle's chimney she thought it would be very nice just to peep inside the door and look at the fire.

So, as Mickle was about to take a bite from the first biscuit, he saw the door slowly open, and the untidy curly head of the little beggar-child come peeping round the corner!

Mickle stared in surprise. The child

177

smiled at him and came right in.

"I'm cold," she said. "I saw the smoke coming from your chimney and I wanted to look at a nice warm fire."

"Come and sit down by it," said Mickle at once. "It's only made of sticks from the woods, but it is cheerful and warm."

So the little ragged girl sat down and warmed her hands. She looked at the bag that Mickle was holding and asked him what was inside it.

"Biscuits," said Mickle.

"Ooh!" said the beggar-child, but she didn't ask for one. Her eyes grew rounder, and she looked small and hungry. Mickle felt that he simply *must* give her a biscuit. So he handed her one.

"Thank you!" said the girl, and crunched it up as quickly as a dog eats a bone! Then she looked hungrily at the bag again.

Mickle knew he shouldn't give her any more because he wouldn't have any for the next five Sundays. But he

found his hand going inside the bag,
and there it was, holding out another
biscuit again!

Well, the girl ate five of those six
biscuits, and Mickle was just handing
her the very last one, when there came
a shout from the gate, "Hi, Binny, hi!
Where are you? Come along at once!"

The beggar-child jumped up. Her
name was Binny, and it was her father
who was calling her. She gave Mickle a
quick hug and flew out into the garden.
Her father was standing by the gate,
waiting.

"This brownie-man has been so kind to me, Father!" cried the little girl. "Give him a reward. Please do!"

She bit her last biscuit and some crumbs fell to the ground beside the gate. The tramp trod them into the earth with his foot and muttered a few strange words. He looked at Mickle out of bright green eyes.

"Sometimes a bit of kindness grows and grows and brings us a reward we don't expect!" he said. "And sometimes it doesn't! But today there is magic in the wind, so maybe you'll be lucky!"

He nodded to Mickle and he and the beggar-child went dancing up the lane together, their rags blowing like dead leaves in the wind. Mickle shut the gate and went back to his warm kitchen. He was hungry – and all his biscuits were gone. Life was very sad.

He forgot all about the tramp and the beggar-child that spring. He never saw them again, and he worked so hard that he really hadn't time to think of anything except food and rest and work.

But one day he noticed a strong little shoot growing by his gatepost. He bent down to look at it. It was not like any seedling he had seen before. Perhaps it was a weed. Mickle thought he would pull it up. Then he thought he wouldn't. So he left it.

And to his enormous surprise it grew and grew very fast indeed, till in three weeks' time it was as high as the top of his gate! It sprouted into leaves. It grew higher still. It grew into a small tree, and Mickle had to walk under it when he went out of the gate. It was really most extraordinary!

He talked to his friends about it. They were used to magic, of course, but no one had ever seen a tree grow quite so quickly.

"It will flower soon and then we shall know what it is," said his friends. And the next week, sure enough, it did flower. It had funny flowers – bright red, with flat yellow middles.

The blossoms didn't last long. The red petals fell off, and the flat yellow middles grew larger. Everyone was most puzzled – till at last Dame Fanny gave a shout and slapped Mickle suddenly on the shoulder.

"It's a biscuit tree! That's what it is! A biscuit tree! Goodness me, one hasn't grown in the kingdom for about five hundred years! A biscuit tree, a biscuit tree!"

Well, Dame Fanny was right. It was a biscuit tree, and no mistake! The biscuits grew till they were ripe, and a sort of sugary powder came over them.

Then they were ready for picking.

And how Mickle enjoyed picking biscuits off his biscuit tree! You would have loved it too. He got some big and little tins from his grocer, lined them

183

with paper, and then picked the
biscuits. He laid each one neatly in a
tin, till the tin was full and he could
put the lid on. Then he took up
another tin and filled that. He did
enjoy himself.

He gave a tin of biscuits to everyone
in the village. This was just like kind
old Mickle, of course. They were pat-a-
cake biscuits, and for a long time
nobody knew why the tree was a pat-a-
cake biscuit tree, nor why it had grown
at all. And then Pixie Lightfoot
suddenly remembered that she had
given Mickle some pat-a-cake biscuits
some months back.

"What did you do with them?" she
asked Mickle. "Did you eat them?"

"No," said Mickle. "I gave them all to
a beggar-child."

184

"Did she drop any crumbs near your gate, where the biscuit tree is growing?" asked Lightfoot.

"Yes – she did – and I remember now, her father stamped them into the ground, and said that sometimes kindness grew its own reward – and he said that there was magic in the wind that day!" cried Mickle.

"Ah – now we know everything!" said Lightfoot. "It was your own bit of kindness that grew! From the biscuit-crumbs came your wonderful tree, Mickle. Oh, how marvellous! I do hope it goes on flowering year after year."

Well, it does, of course, so Mickle always has plenty of biscuits to eat, sell, or give away. Go by his gate in Misty Village during the summer and see his biscuits growing on the tree – he'll be sure to give you a pocketful if you wish him good morning!

The Man Who Wasn't Father Christmas

There was once an old man with a long white beard who loved children. He was very poor, so he couldn't give the children anything, and you can guess that he always wished at Christmas-time that he was Father Christmas.

"Goodness! What fun I'd have if I were Father Christmas!" he thought. "Think of having a sack that was always full of toys – that couldn't be emptied, because it was magic. How happy I should be!"

Now one Christmas-time the old man saw a little notice in the window of a big shop. This is what is said:

WANTED! A man with a white beard to be FATHER CHRISTMAS, and give out paper leaflets in the street.

Well, the old man stared at this

186

notice, and wondered if he could get the job. How lovely to dress up as Father Christmas, and go up and down the streets with all the children staring at him! He would be so happy.

So he marched into the shop and asked if he could have the job.

"The work is not hard," said the shopman. "All you have to do is to dress up in a red cloak and trousers and big boots, and take a sack with you."

"Will it be full of toys?" asked the old man, his eyes shining at the thought.

WANTED!
A man with a white beard to be FATHER CHRISTMAS, and give out paper leaflets in the street.

"Of course not!" said the shopman. "It will be full of leaflets for you to give to the passers-by. I have had these leaflets printed to tell everyone to come to our shop this Christmas and buy their presents here. I thought it would be a good idea to dress somebody up as Father Christmas, and let him give out the leaflets."

"I see," said the old man. "I rather thought it would be nice to give the children something."

"Well, what an idea!" said the shop-

188

man. "Now, see if this red Father Christmas costume fits you."

It fitted the old man well. He got into it and looked at himself in the glass. He really looked exactly like old Father Christmas. His long white beard flowed down over his chest and his bright blue eyes twinkled brightly.

He took his sack of leaflets and went out. It was the day before Christmas and everyone was busy shopping. How the children stared when they saw the old man walking along in the road.

"It's Father Christmas!" they shouted. "It's Father Christmas! Come and see him!"

Soon the children were crowding round the old man, asking if they could peep into his sack. But alas, there were no toys there, and all he had to give the children were the leaflets. The children were disappointed.

"Fancy Father Christmas only giving us leaflets about Mr White's shop," they said. "We thought he was a kind old man – but he isn't. He didn't even give us a sweet."

The old man heard the children

saying these things and he was sad. "I made a mistake in taking this job," he said to himself. "It is horrid to pretend to be somebody kind and not be able to give the boys and girls even a penny! I feel dreadful!"

It began to snow. The old man plodded along the streets, giving out his leaflets. And suddenly he heard a curious sound. It was the sound of bells!

"Where are those bells, I wonder?" thought the old man, looking all round. "It sounds like horse-bells. But everyone has cars nowadays. There are no horses in this town."

It wasn't horse-bells he heard. It was reindeer-bells! To the great surprise of the old man, a large sleigh drove down the road, drawn by reindeer. And in it was – well, you can guess without being told – the real Father Christmas!

The sleigh drew up, and Father Christmas leaned out. "Am I anywhere near the town of Up-and-Down?" he called.

Then he stared hard at the old man –

191

and he frowned. "You look like *me*!" he said. "Why are you dressed like that?"

"Well, just to get a job of work," said the old man. "But really because I love children, and I thought if I dressed up like you, they would think I *was* you, and would come round me and be happy. But all I have in my sack is stupid leaflets about somebody's shop – I haven't any toys to give away, as you have. So instead of making the children happy I have disappointed them. I am sorry now I ever took this job."

"Well, well, you did it for the best," said Father Christmas, smiling suddenly. "I like people who love children. They are always the nicest people, you know. Look here – would you like to do me a good turn?"

"I'd love to," said the old man.

"Well," said Father Christmas, "I haven't had any tea, and I feel so hungry and thirsty. Would you mind taking care of my reindeer for me while I'm in a tea shop? They don't like standing still, so you'll have to

drive them round and round the town. And if you meet any children, you must do exactly as I always do."

"What's that?" asked the old man, his eyes shining.

"You must stop, and say to them, "A happy Christmas to you! What would you like out of my sack?" And you must let the child dip its hand into my sack and take out what it wants. You won't mind doing that, will you? I always do that as I drive along."

"Mind doing that! It would be the

thing I would like best in the world," said the old man, hardly believing his ears. "It's – it's – it's – well, I just can't tell you how happy it will make me. I can't believe it's true!"

Father Christmas smiled his wide smile. He jumped down from the sleigh and threw the reins to the old man.

"Come back in an hour," he said. "I'll have finished my tea by then."

He went into a tea shop. The old man climbed into the driving-seat. He was trembling with joy. He looked at the enormous sack beside him on the seat. It was simply bursting with toys! He cracked the whip and the reindeer set off with a jingling of bells.

Soon they met three children. How those children stared! Then they went quite mad with delight and yelled to the old man: "Father Christmas! Father Christmas! Stop a minute, do!"

The old man stopped the reindeer. He beamed at the children. "A happy Christmas to you!" he said. "What would you like out of my sack?"

"An engine, please," said the boy.

"A doll, please," said one of the girls.

"A book, please," said another girl.

"Dip into my sack and find what you want," said the old man. And with shining faces the three children dipped in their hands . . . and pulled out exactly what they wanted! They rushed home with shouts of joy.

Well, the old man stopped at every child he met, wished them a happy Christmas, and asked them what they wanted. And dozens of happy children

dipped into the enormous sack and pulled out just what they longed for.

At the end of an hour the old man drove the reindeer back to the tea shop. Father Christmas was waiting, putting on his big fur gloves. He smiled when he saw the bright face of the old man.

"You've had a good time, I can see," he said. "Thanks so much. I don't give presents to grown-ups usually – but you might hang up your stocking just for fun tonight. Goodbye!"

He drove off with a ringing of sleigh-bells. The old man went back to the shop in a happy dream, took off his red clothes and went home.

"I've never been so happy before," he said as he got into bed. "Never! If only people knew how wonderful it is to give happiness to others! How lucky Father Christmas is to go about the world giving presents to all the boys and girls!"

The old man hung up his stocking, though he felt rather ashamed of it. And when he woke up in the morning, what do you think was in it?

A magic purse was in it – a purse that was always full of pennies! No matter how many were taken out, there were always some left.

"A penny-purse – a magic penny-purse!" cried the old man joyfully. "My word – what fun I'll have with the children now!"

He does – for he always has a penny to give each one. I wonder if you've ever seen the little penny-purse. It is black and has two letters in silver on the front. They are 'F.C.' I expect you can guess what they stand for!

The Goblin Aeroplane

"It's such a lovely day you can take your work books on to the hillside, if you like," said Mummy one morning to Jill and Robert.

So out they went.

"What have you got to do?" Robert asked Jill.

"I've got to learn how to spell six words," said Jill. "They're rather hard. Here they are: mushroom, toadstool, honey, dewdrop, magic and enchantment. Don't you think they are hard, Robert?"

"Yes," said Robert. "I'm sure I don't know how to spell them. I've got to learn my seven times table."

"I'm only up to five times," said Jill. "Ooh, isn't it lovely out on the hillside, Robert?"

The two children sat down and opened their books – but it was hard to work. First a lovely peacock butterfly flew by. Then a tiny copper beetle with a shining back ran over Jill's book. Then a robin came and sat so near to them that they hardly dared to move in case he was frightened away.

"I say, Jill!" said Robert at last. "How much work have you done?"

"None!" said Jill. "Have you learned your table, Robert?"

"Only as far as two times seven," answered Robert. "It's a pity to have to do homework when the sun is shining so brightly and we'd like to play."

200

"Well, let's not do it," said Jill. "No one will know, because we can take our books to bed with us tonight, and after Mummy has gone we can get them out and learn our words and do our tables then!"

"Oh no, Jill!" said Robert, shocked. "Mummy trusted us to do our lessons here, and we must. It would be mean to play when she sent us out here for a treat."

"All right," said Jill. "It would be mean – so let's get on quickly and finish them, Robert."

The two children turned their backs on one another, put their fingers in their ears and began to learn their spelling and tables. They didn't look up once, even when the robin flew down at their feet. They meant to do their lessons really well.

Soon Jill sat up.

"I've finished, Robert!" she said. "Hear my spelling, will you?"

"Yes, if you'll hear my seven times table," said Robert. They passed each other their books, and Jill was just beginning to spell "mushroom" when a very strange thing happened.

They saw a tiny speck in the sky, which rapidly grew larger. It was bright red and yellow.

"It's an aeroplane, Jill!" said Robert. "But what a funny one!"

It certainly was odd, for instead of having flat wings like an ordinary aeroplane, it had curved wings like a bird, and it flapped these slowly up and down as it flew.

"It's coming down!" said Jill, in

excitement. "Ooh, look, Robert, it's coming down quite near us!"

Sure enough the strange aeroplane flew swiftly towards them, flapping its odd red and yellow wings. From the cockpit a funny little man peeped out. He waved his hand to them.

The aeroplane suddenly dipped downwards, and with a whirr of wings that sounded rather like a giant bee buzzing, it landed on the hillside near the excited children. They ran up to it in astonishment.

"What a tiny aeroplane!" cried Robert. "I've never seen one like that before!"

"It's a goblin aeroplane!" said the pilot inside, peeping at them and grinning widely. "It belongs to me."

"Are you a goblin then?" asked Jill, in surprise.

"Of course," said the strange pilot, and he jumped out of his plane. Then the children saw that he really was a goblin. His ears were pointed and stuck out above his cap.

His body was round and fat, and his feet were as pointed as his ears.

"I've come to ask if you can tell me where Greenfield Farm is," he said.

"Oh yes," said Robert. "It's over that field, then through a path in the wood, then over a stile, then down by the stream, then over the little hill, then—"

"Goodness!" cried the goblin, "I shall never find it in my aeroplane! Can't you tell me how to get to it from the air?"

"I might, if I were in your aeroplane with you," said Robert, doubtfully. "I think I should know what the farm looks like, but I couldn't quite tell you how to go. You see, I've never been in an aeroplane."

"Well, come for a ride in mine," said the goblin, grinning. "You and your sister can both come, and as soon as you show me Greenfield Farm and I

205

land there, you can hop out and run home again."

"Ooh!" shouted both children in excitement, and they danced up and down with glee. "Do you really mean it?"

"Of course," said the goblin. "Come on, hop in."

So they climbed into the aeroplane, and the goblin climbed in too. Jill and Robert looked to see how he flew it. It was a very strange aeroplane, there was no doubt of that. In front of the goblin's seat were dozens of little buttons, each with something printed on. One had "Down" on, one had "Up", and another had "Sideways". Still another had "Home" on, and a fifth had "Fast", and a sixth one "Slow". There were many more besides.

The goblin pressed the button marked "Up" and the aeroplane began to flap its strange wings. It rose from the ground, and the children clutched the sides in excitement, for it was a very odd feeling to be in something that flapped its wings and flew into the air.

"There's the farm!" cried Robert, and he pointed to a pretty farmhouse over to the east. At once the goblin pressed a button marked "East", and the aeroplane flapped its way to the right. Soon it was over the farm, but to the children's great surprise it didn't

land, but flew straight on.

"Aren't you going to land?" asked Jill. "You've passed right over the farm."

"Ha, ha!" laughed the goblin, and it was such a nasty laugh that the children looked at him in surprise.

"Why don't you land?" asked Robert. "I don't want to go too far, you know, because of getting home again."

"You're going to come with me!" said the goblin. "You didn't suppose I really wanted to go to the farm, did you? Why, that was only a trick to get you both into my aeroplane!"

The children sat silent for a minute,

they were so surprised. Jill felt
frightened.

"What do you want us for?" asked
Robert at last.

"To sell to Big-One the giant," said
the goblin. "He's lonely in his castle
and he wants two children to talk to."

"But, gosh, you can't do a thing like
that!" cried Robert, in a rage. "Take us
back home at once, or I'll make you
very sorry for yourself!"

The goblin smiled a wide smile, and

said nothing. Robert wondered what to do. He did not dare to hit the goblin, for he was afraid that the aeroplane might fall. So he just sat there frowning, holding Jill's hand tightly, for he saw that she was frightened.

After about twenty minutes Robert looked over the side of the aeroplane. Far below was a strange-looking country with palaces gleaming on hills, and castles towering high.

"It must be Fairyland," whispered Jill when Robert pointed it out to her. "Oh, Robert, this is a great adventure, even if that old goblin is taking us to a giant!"

Just then the aeroplane plunged downwards, for the goblin had pressed the button marked "Down". It flew to a great castle standing on a mountain top, and landed on one of the towers. The goblin leaped out and ran to a staircase leading down from the roof.

"Hey, Big-One!" he called. "Here are two children for you! Where's that sack of gold you promised me?"

Robert and Jill heard great footsteps

coming up the stairs, and a giant's head peeped out on to the roof. He had a huge head of hair, a turned-up nose, a wide mouth and very nice blue eyes as big as dinner plates. The children liked the look of him much better than they liked the goblin.

"So these are the children," said the giant, in a loud booming voice. "Well, they look all right, goblin. You can have your sack of gold tonight. I haven't any by me at the moment. Come for it at six o'clock."

"All right," said the goblin, and he went back to the aeroplane.

"Climb out," he ordered, and Robert and Jill climbed down from the cockpit, feeling very strange. The goblin leaped into his seat, pressed the button marked "Up" and disappeared into the sky, shouting that he would be back at six o'clock without fail for his sack of gold.

The giant looked at the two children.

"Will you come down into my kitchen?" he said, in a kind voice. "I am sure you want something to eat and drink after your ride."

Robert and Jill felt glad to hear him speak so politely. He couldn't be very fierce, they thought. They followed him down the stairs and came to a vast kitchen where a huge kettle boiled loudly on a fire.

"Sit down," said Big-One, and he pointed to two chairs. But neither Robert nor Jill could climb on to the seats, for they were so high up. So the giant gently lifted them up, and then took the boiling kettle from the fire.

He made some cocoa in three china

cups, and set out three enormous plates, on each of which he had placed a very large slice of currant cake.

"Please join me in a little snack," he said. "It is really very kind of you to take pity on me and come to live with me. I didn't think any children would be willing to come here, you know."

"Why, we weren't willing!" said Robert, in astonishment. "The goblin got us here by a trick. We didn't want to come here at all!"

"What!" cried the giant, upsetting his cocoa in his surprise. "Do you mean to say that nasty little goblin brought you here against your will?"

"Yes," said Robert, and he told Big-One all about the morning's happenings.

Jill listened and nodded her head, eating her currant cake, which was really most delicious.

The giant was terribly upset when he heard about the trick that the goblin had played on the children.

"I don't know what to do!" he said, and two big tears stood in his saucer-eyes. "I wouldn't have had such a thing happen for the world! Now, however can I get you back again? And, oh dear me, that nasty goblin will be coming for his sack of gold too, and I haven't any. You see, I thought you'd be able to help me with my spells, for children are very clever, much cleverer than stupid giants like me. I thought I'd get you to help me with a gold-spell, and make some gold before the evening."

214

"Well, we don't mind helping you a bit," said Robert, who liked the big giant very much. "Don't cry. You've splashed a tear into your cocoa, and it will make it taste salty."

"Will you really help me?" cried Big-One. "Oh, you good, kind children! Well, I'll just clear away these things and then we'll set about making a gold-spell."

He put the cups and plates into a huge sink and washed them up. Then he took the children into a big bare room with many chalk circles drawn on the floor. A pot hung over a fire that burned with strange green flames.

"Now first of all I've got to write six words in the biggest of these chalk circles," he said. "But, oh dear me, I don't know how to spell them! Still, children are very clever, so I do hope you'll be able to help me. Can either of you spell 'mushroom'?"

"I can!" cried Jill, excitedly. "I learned it this morning! M-U-S-H-R-O-O-M!"

The giant carefully wrote it down in the circle as Jill spelled it. Then he looked up at her.

"Now could you spell 'magic'?" he asked.

"Yes!" said Jill, "M-A-G-I-C! That was one of the words I had to learn this morning, too!"

Well, would you believe it, all the words that the giant needed for his spells were the very ones Jill had to learn! Wasn't it a good thing she had done them so well? The last one the giant wanted was "enchantment".

"That's the hardest one," said Jill, and she frowned. "Oh, I do hope I remember it properly. Let me see. E-N-"

"Where's your spelling book, Jill?" asked Robert, terribly afraid that Jill might spell the word wrong after all. "You could look it up before you spell it."

"We left both our books on the hillside!" said Jill. "No, I must try and spell it out of my head. Let me think for a minute – yes, I think I've got it. E-N-C-H-A-N-T-M-E-N-T!"

Big-One wrote it carefully down. Then he drew a toadstool and a mushroom right in the very middle of the circle, put a spot of honey on each, and shook a dewdrop from a piece of grass on to the honey.

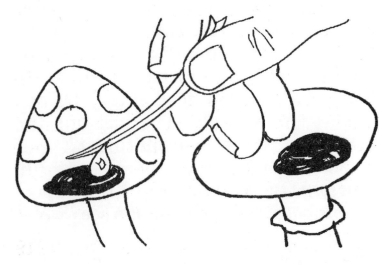

"That's all ready for the spell now!" he said. "What a good thing you knew how to spell mushroom, toadstool, honey, dewdrop, magic and enchant- ment, Jill. But, oh dear me – the next thing we have to do is very hard!"

"What's that?" asked Robert.

"Well, two of us have to dance round the circle holding hands," said the giant, "while one stands in the middle chanting the seven times table. But I don't know the seven times table. I only know twice times."

"I don't know it either," said Jill.

"But I do!" cried Robert. "I learned it this morning. I can say it! I'll be the one to stand in the middle."

"Oh, good!" said Big-One, and he rubbed his great hands together in delight. "Now listen – Jill and I will dance round together, and you must stand still in the middle saying your seven times table at the top of your voice. At the end of it I have to say twelve magic words, and then, if we've

done the spell right, a sack of gold appears right in the middle of the circle!"

"Come on, let's do it!" cried Jill. "Are you sure you know all your seven times perfectly, Robert? It might spoil the spell if you got something wrong."

"I'm not quite sure of twelve times seven," said Robert. "I think it's eighty-four, but just wait a minute and I'll work it out to make sure."

He took a piece of the giant's chalk and wrote the figure 12 seven times on the floor. Then he added them up, and sure enough, it made eighty-four, so he was quite right.

Then they started the spell. Jill and the giant danced round the circle, and

Robert stood in the middle saying his seven times table at the top of his voice. When he had finished, the giant shouted out a string of curious magic words, and all the words he had written inside the circle suddenly vanished!

Then *crash*! A great sack suddenly appeared in the middle of the circle and knocked Robert down. He was up in a minute, and peeped into the mouth of the sack.

"Yes, the spell has worked!" he cried. "It's full of gold! Ooh, what powerful magic! And what a good job I knew my seven times table properly!"

The giant was so pleased. He could hardly thank Robert and Jill enough.

"You don't know how grateful I am

to you," he said. "I can pay that horrid goblin now, though I don't think he deserves a penny, because he brought you here by a trick. But the next thing is – how am I going to get you home again?"

"I don't know," said Robert. "Could you use magic, do you think?"

"No," said Big-One. "I don't know any that would take you home. Wait a minute – let me think."

He sat down on a stool and frowned for five minutes. Then he jumped up and clapped his hands so loudly that it quite frightened Jill.

"I've a wonderful plan!" he said. "The goblin will come in his aeroplane tonight at six o'clock. Now listen – I'll hide you behind a chimney pot on the roof of the castle. When the goblin arrives I'll call him downstairs to the cellar to fetch his gold. As soon as he's gone down the stairs you must pop out, jump into the aeroplane and fly home!"

"But we don't know how to fly a goblin aeroplane!" said Robert.

"Oh, it's quite easy," said Big-One. "Didn't you see all those buttons? Well, you just press the one that says 'Up' and then the one that says 'Home', and then the one that says 'Down' when you see your home, and there you are!"

"Well, I think I could do that," said Robert. "Anyway, I'll try. But what shall we do until six o'clock?"

"Perhaps you'd like to come out with me in my yellow motor-car and see the sights of Fairyland?" said the giant.

"Ooh, yes!" cried the children. So the giant took them out to his great motor-car, and they climbed into it. What a time they had! They saw elves and

fairies, brownies and gnomes, pixies and witches, and all kinds of strange little folk. They went into glittering palaces, they had dinner with a wizard and tea with a brownie, so you can guess what a glorious day they had. They were sorry when half-past five came, and the giant took them back to his castle.

He took them up to the roof and showed them a chimney to hide behind. Then he shook hands with both of them, and thanked them very much for all their help.

"Thank you for the lovely day you've

given us," said the children. "We only wish we could stay longer, but our mother would be worried if we did."

"Shh! Here comes the goblin!" said Big-One, suddenly. He ran down the stairs, and the children were left alone behind the chimney. They heard a whirring sound, and saw the red and yellow aeroplane flying down, its strange wings flapping as it came.

The goblin landed neatly on the roof and ran to the stairs.

"Where's my sack of gold, Big-One?" he cried.

"Come down and fetch it!" came the giant's booming voice. "It's in my cellar."

The goblin raced down the stairs. As soon as he was gone Robert and Jill ran to the aeroplane and climbed into it. Robert pressed the button marked "Up", and the aeroplane at once rose upwards. Then he pressed the button marked "Home", and the machine turned round in the air and flew steadily towards the setting sun.

Jill looked back and saw the goblin standing on the roof of the castle, shouting wildly. The giant stood beside him, laughing. They could hear his great "Ho-ho-ho" for a long way.

The aeroplane flew steadily onwards. Suddenly Jill gave a cry and pointed downwards.

"There's our house, Robert!" she cried. "Press the 'Down' button, quickly!"

Robert pressed it. The aeroplane swooped down and landed on the hillside where the children had sat learning their lessons that morning.

Robert and Jill jumped out, picked up their books which were still where they had left them, and raced home.

"Why, my dears, wherever have you been?" cried their mother. "I have been so worried about you!"

"Oh Mummy, we've had such an adventure!" cried Robert. "We've been up in a goblin aeroplane!" and he told her all that happened. Their mother was so astonished that she simply couldn't say a word.

"Come and see the aeroplane," said Robert. "It's out on the hillside."

They all three ran to the hill – but just as they got there they heard a whirring sound and Robert pointed up in the air.

"There it goes!" he cried. "I expect it's gone back to the goblin. Oh, Mummy, I wish you'd seen all the buttons inside, and had come for a ride with us."

"But that's not an aeroplane," said their mother. "It's only a very big bird. I can see its wings flapping."

"No, really, it's the goblin aeroplane," said Jill. But I don't think their mother believed it.

"Anyhow, my dears," she said, as they all went home again, "what a very good thing it was that you were good and learned your lessons properly this morning – else you might have had to stay with that giant!"

And it was a good thing, wasn't it?

The Boy With a Thousand Wishes

There was once a sharp boy called Gordon. He longed and longed to meet a brownie or a pixie, or someone belonging to the little folk, because he wanted to ask for a wish.

"Just one wish," said Gordon to himself. "Only just one! Surely they wouldn't mind me having just one."

Well, his chance came one morning when he was walking so quietly that a brownie who was sitting under a bush, half asleep, didn't see him until Gordon was right on top of him. The brownie tried to scramble away into the bush – but Gordon put out a long arm and caught him.

"A brownie at last!" said Gordon, pleased. "Good! No – it's no use struggling – you can't get away!"

The brownie stopped struggling at once. He was a tiny fellow, only just as high as Gordon's knee, and his eyes were as green as moss in the sunlight. His beard almost reached the ground.

"Let me go," begged the brownie.

"What will you give me if I do?" asked Gordon, keeping a tight hold of the little fellow.

"What do you want?" asked the green-eyed brownie sulkily.

"I want a wish," said Gordon firmly.

"A wish! Just one wish?" said the brownie in surprise. "Most people ask for three."

"One wish will do very well for me," said Gordon. The brownie stood straight up and looked closely into Gordon's eyes.

"Take my advice and do not ask for a wish," he said. "You'll be sorry!"

"I want a wish," said Gordon. He shook the little fellow hard. "Now, hurry up, or I'll take you home with me."

"You can have your wish," said the brownie, and his eyes gleamed like green stones. "Let me go!"

"Not till I've wished my wish!" said Gordon. "And this is what I wish – that I may have a wish granted every hour of the day and night!"

The brownie pulled himself free and began to laugh. "You think you're clever, but you're not!" he called in his high little voice. "Have all your wishes – but you'll be sorry!"

He disappeared behind a tree. Gordon rubbed his hands in glee. He felt quite sure that he would never be sorry.

"I wonder nobody has ever thought of this before!" he said to himself as he went home. "One magic wish can bring as many other wishes as I like! Why people ask for three and then just use them for three silly things and no more puzzles me! Now I can have a wish granted every single hour!"

It was a long way home, and Gordon felt tired. He stood still and thought. "I don't see why I shouldn't have my first wish now!" he said. "Well – I wish for a fine motor-car to take me home!"

There was a bang – and out of the air appeared a red motor-car! At the wheel sat a fat gnome with a most unpleasant face. He grinned at Gordon.

"Good morning!" he said. "I'm your wish-gnome. I have to grant you a wish every single hour. The very first time you forget I'll take you off with me, and you shall be my slave! Then you will have to do my wishes!"

"You be careful, or I'll wish you away!" said Gordon sharply.

"Well, if you do that, your wishes won't come true any more, because I'm the fellow that grants them!" said the gnome. "Now hop in and I'll take you home!"

Gordon hopped in. He thought it was a pity that he had to have a wish-gnome to grant his wishes. When he got home his mother and father, brothers and sisters were most astonished to hear his story and see his fine new car.

"Wish me a silk dress!" cried Elaine.

"Wish me a car like yours!" cried John.

"Wish me, wish me, wish me . . ." shouted everyone.

"I'll wish what I like," said Gordon. "Be quiet, everyone! I shall have twenty-four wishes each day and night, and I will wish us riches, a castle, servants and anything else we want. This gnome is my wish-gnome and he has to grant all my wishes!"

Well, all that day, each hour that came, Gordon wished. He wished for a castle. *Bang!* It appeared on the hill nearby! The whole family went to see it and chose their own rooms.

He wished for servants. *Bang!* They all appeared, one after the other, bowing low. He wished for money to buy fine food. *Bang!* A great purse of gold appeared in his hand, and Gordon sent the servants out to buy meat, fish, eggs, cakes, biscuits – everything he could think of! What a feast they all had!

By the time it was eight o'clock, Gordon had the castle, servants, gold, fine suits and dresses for everyone, a car for each of them, a throne of gold, and a bed of silver. He had never felt so grand in all his life.

He was very tired with all the excitement. "I'm going to bed," he said to the wish-gnome. "Wake me at eight o'clock tomorrow."

"But you have to wish a wish each hour of the night!" said the gnome. "Don't you remember that you wished for a wish to be granted every single hour of the day and night?"

"Good gracious! Surely you don't mean

I've got to wake up every hour and wish!" cried Gordon. "I'll save them all up and wish twelve wishes tomorrow morning."

"Oh no, you won't," said the gnome with a grin. "You'll just keep to what you said. I'll wake you up each hour to wish."

So poor Gordon had to wake up each hour and wish something. He was so sleepy that it was difficult to think of things. He wished for a golden bicycle, a cat with blue eyes, a goldfish in a big bowl, three singing birds, and many other things.

The next day he went on wishing. He wished himself a crown. He wished himself a kingdom. He wished his mother a golden ring with big diamonds in it. He wished his father a pipe rimmed with precious stones.

His brothers and sisters quarrelled about his wishes. They were always wanting him to wish something for them, and they could never wait their turn.

"Oh, do stop quarrelling!" begged Gordon. "I should have thought that

being so rich, and having such wonderful things to wear and to eat, you would have been very happy. Instead, you quarrel and fight, and disturb me all the time."

It was such a nuisance having to wake up each night and wish every hour. "I really can't be bothered to wake up tonight," said Gordon to the wish-gnome one night. "I'll go without my wishes."

"Gordon, if you do that, you'll be in my power and I'll whisk you away!" cried the gnome in delight.

Gordon looked at the gnome. He couldn't bear him. "How can I get rid of you?" he asked. "I really don't feel as if I want anything else now, and it's a great nuisance to have to think of a wish every hour!"

"You can only get rid of me if you ask me to do something I can't do!" said the wish-gnome, grinning. "But as I can grant every wish, it's not likely you'll be able to do that. I shall just stay with you till you get so tired of wishing that you'll stop – and then I shall whisk you away and make you do my wishes."

So poor Gordon went on and on wishing each day and night. He longed to get rid of the gnome. He set him all kinds of impossible things to do – but the gnome did them all!

Gordon wished for seven blue elephants with yellow ears. He was sure there were none in the world! But the gnome brought them all right, and very peculiar they looked, standing in the courtyard, waving their blue trunks about!

It didn't matter what the boy wished, his wishes came true. And all the time his family squabbled and fought, each trying to get Gordon's wishes for themselves.

"Wish me a new white horse!" screamed Fanny.

"Wish me three black dogs!" shouted Ken.

"Wish me a more comfortable bed!" cried Elaine.

"You be quiet, Elaine! It's my turn to

have a wish!" said John fiercely, and he pulled Elaine's hair. She slapped his face. He ran after her, and she bumped into Gordon, knocking him down. John trod on him.

Gordon leaped to his feet in a rage. "How dare you! How dare you!" he yelled. "I'm a king! I won't have you treating me like this!"

"Pooh! You're only Gordon, really!" said Elaine rudely.

"Oh, I am, am I?" said Gordon fiercely. "Well, you're only Elaine. I wish all my wishes undone! May everything be as it was before! I'm tired of all this!"

Bang! The castle vanished. The servants disappeared. Their rich clothes became the poor ones of before. The whole family found themselves in their cottage, staring in fear and surprise at one another.

"Serves you right!" said Gordon. "You don't deserve good fortune. You were much nicer when you were poor and hard-working. And so was I!"

He sat with his head in his hand,

unhappy and puzzled. To think that he
had all the wishes in the world and yet
was not so happy as when he had none!
It was too bad.

In an hour's time the wish-gnome
appeared, grinning. "Well!" he said.
"Do you want to wish your castle back?"

"No, I don't," said Gordon. He snatched a boiling kettle off the stove. "Freeze this boiling water!" he said. "Go on! I'm hot and I want ice to suck. Freeze this hot water."

Well, the gnome did everything he could to make that water freeze, but of course he couldn't. No one can make hot water into ice – it just won't happen!

The gnome threw down the kettle,

looking angry. "It can't be done!" he said. "It's impossible. Wish something else that I can do, or I shall disappear for ever and you won't be able to have another wish come true all your life long."

"Then disappear!" cried Gordon. "Go! I don't want any more wishes!"

Bang! The gnome went – and that was the last time Gordon ever saw him. No more of his wishes came true – but he didn't care! It was a better thing to live happily in a cottage with his family, and to work hard, and laugh, than to live in a huge castle with nothing to do but quarrel and fight.

"I thought I was so sharp, only asking for one wish in order to have thousands," said Gordon to himself. "But I was stupid! I'll never do it again."

He needn't worry. He won't get the chance!

The
Witch's Cat

Old Dame Kirri was a witch. You could tell she was because she had bright green eyes. She was a good witch though, and spent most of her time making good spells to help people who were ill or unhappy.

She lived in Toppling Cottage, which was just like its name and looked exactly as if it was going to topple over. But it was kept up by strong magic and not a brick had fallen, although the cottage was five hundred years old.

At the back of the cottage was the witch's garden. Round it ran a very, very high wall, taller than the tallest man.

"I like a high wall. It keeps people from peeping and prying," said old witch Kirri. "In my garden I grow a lot of strange and powerful herbs. I don't want people to see them and steal them. I won't have people making spells from my magic herbs – they might make bad ones."

The witch had a cat. It was black and big, and had green eyes very like the witch's. Its name was Cinder-Boy.

Cinder-Boy helped the witch with her spells. He was really a remarkably clever cat. He knew how to sit exactly in the middle of a chalk ring without moving, while Kirri the witch danced round and sang spells. He knew how to go out and collect dewdrops in the moonlight. He took a special little silver cup for that, and never spilled a drop.

He never drank milk. He liked tea, made as strong as the witch made for herself. Sometimes he would sit and sip his tea and purr, and the witch would sip her tea and purr, too. It was funny to see them.

Cinder-Boy loved to sleep in the walled-in garden. He knew all the flowers and herbs which grew there. No weeds were allowed to grow. Cinder-Boy scratched them all up.

But one day he came to a small plant growing at the foot of the wall. It had leaves like a rose-tree. It had pale pink flowers, with a mass of yellow stamens in the middle. It smelled very sweet.

"What flower are you?" said Cinder-Boy. "You smell rather like a rose."

"Well, that's just what I am," said the plant. "I'm a wild rose."

"How did you get here?" said Cinder-Boy, surprised.

"A bird dropped a seed," said the wild rose. "But I don't like being here, black cat."

"My name is Cinder-Boy," said the

witch's cat. "Why don't you like being here? It is a very nice place to be."

"Well, I feel shut in," said the wild rose. "I'm not very large. If I was taller than the wall I could grow up into the air, and see over the top. I don't like being down here at the bottom, shut in."

"Well, grow tall then," said Cinder-Boy. "I can give you a spell to make your stems nice and long, if you like. Then you can reach up to the top of the wall and look over. There's a nice view there, I can tell you."

247

"Oh, would you do that?" said the wild rose in delight. "Thank you!"

So Cinder-Boy went off to get a spell which would make the stems of the wild rose grow very long. He soon found one. It was in a small blue bottle, and he poured it into a watering-can. The spell was blue, too.

Then he watered the wild rose with the spell, and it began to work almost at once. In two or three days the stems of

the wild rose plant had grown quite high into the air.

"Go on growing. You will soon be at the top of the wall!" said Cinder-Boy. So the wild rose went on, making its stems longer and longer, hoping to get to the very top of the wall.

But when Cinder-Boy next strolled out into the garden to see how it was getting on, what a shock he had! Every single stem was bent over and lay sprawling over the grass!

"Why, what has happened?" said Cinder-Boy, waving his tail in surprise.

"My stalks grew tall, but they didn't grow strong," said the wild rose, sadly. "Just as I reached the top of the wall, they all flopped over and fell down. They are not strong enough to bear their own weight."

"Well, how do plants with weak stems manage to climb high then?" said Cinder-Boy, puzzled. "Runner beans grow high and they have very weak stems. Sweet-peas grow high, and they have weak stems too. I'll go and see how they do it."

So off he went, for the witch grew both in the garden. He soon came back.

"The beans twine their stalks round poles," he said, "and the sweetpeas grow little green fingers, called tendrils, which catch hold of things, and they pull themselves up high like that. Can't you do that?"

The wild rose couldn't. It didn't know how to. Its stems wouldn't twist themselves, however much it tried to make them do so. And it couldn't grow a tendril at all.

"Well, we must think of another way," said the cat.

"Cinder-Boy, how do you get up to the top of the wall?" asked the wild rose. "You are often up there in the sun. I see you. Well, how do you get to the top?"

"I run up the trees," said Cinder-Boy. "Do you see the young fruit-trees near you? Well, I run up those to the top of the wall. I use my claws to help me. I dig them into the bark of the trees, and hold on with them."

He showed the wild rose his big curved

claws. "I can put them in or out as I like," he said. "They are very useful claws."

The wild rose thought they were too. "If I grew claws like that I could easily climb up the fruit-trees, right through them to the top, and then I'd be waving at the top of the wall," it said. "Can't you get me some claws like yours, Cinder-Boy?"

The cat blinked his green eyes and thought hard. "I know what I could do," he said. "I could ask the witch

Kirri, my mistress, to make some magic claws that would grow on you. I'll ask her today. In return you must promise to grow her some lovely scarlet rosehips which she can trim her hats and bonnets with in the autumn."

"Oh, I will, I will," promised the wild rose. So Cinder-Boy went off to the witch Kirri and asked her for what he wanted.

She grumbled a little. "It is difficult to make claws," she said. "Very difficult. You will have to help me, Cinder-Boy. You will have to sit in the middle of a blue ring of chalk, and put out all your claws at once, while I sing a magic song. Don't be scared at what happens."

In the middle of the garden the witch drew a chalk ring and Cinder-Boy went to sit in the middle of it. He stuck out all his claws as she commanded and she danced round with her broomstick singing such a magic song that Cinder-Boy felt quite scared. Then a funny thing happened.

His claws fell out on to the ground with a clatter – and they turned red or

green as they fell. He looked at his paws and saw new ones growing. Then those fell out, too. How very, very strange!

Soon there was quite a pile of claws on the ground. Then the witch stopped singing and dancing, and rubbed out the ring of chalk.

"You can come out now, Cinder-Boy," she said. "The magic is finished."

Cinder-Boy collected all the red and green claws. They were strong and curved and sharp. He took them to the bottom of the garden, and came to the wild rose.

"I've got claws for you!" he said. "The witch Kirri did some strong magic. Look, here they are. I'll press each one into your stems, till you have claws all down them. Then I'll say a growing spell, and they will grow into you properly and belong to you."

So Cinder-Boy did that, and the wild rose felt the cat-claws growing firmly into the long stems.

"Now," said Cinder-Boy, in excitement, "now you will be able to climb up through the fruit-tree, wild rose. I will help you at first."

So Cinder-Boy took the wild rose stems, all set with claws, and pushed them up into the little fruit-tree that grew near by. The claws took hold of the bark and held on firmly. Soon all the stems were climbing up high through the little fruit tree, the claws digging themselves into the trunk and the branches.

The wild rose grew higher. It pulled itself up by its new claws. It was soon at the top of the wall! It could see right over it to the big world beyond.

"Now I'm happy!" said the wild rose to Cinder-Boy. "Come and sit up here on the wall beside me. Let us look at the big world together. Oh, Cinder-Boy, it is lovely up here. I am not shut in any longer. Thank you for my claws. I do hope I shall go on growing them now."

It did. And it grew beautiful scarlet berries in the autumn, for witch Kirri's

255

winter bonnets. You should see how pretty they are when she trims them with the rosehips!

Ever since that day the wild roses have grown cats' claws all down their stems, sometimes green and sometimes red or pink. They use them to climb with. Have you seen them? If you haven't, do go and look. It will surprise you to see cats' claws growing out of a plant!

It was a good idea of Cinder-Boy's, wasn't it?

The
Walkaway Shoes

"You know, the two new brownies who have set up a shop in Toadstool Cottage make the most beautiful shoes," said Pixie Light-Feet to Limpy the gnome. "You should get them to make you a pair of shoes for your poor old feet, Limpy. Then you could walk well again."

Limpy went to see the two brownies, Slick and Sharpy. They bowed and smiled and welcomed him.

"Yes, yes, Limpy. We will make you such a comfortable pair of shoes that you won't want to take them off even when you go to bed!" they said.

Well, they made him a red pair with green laces, and they were so beautiful and so comfortable that Limpy went around telling everyone about them.

Soon all the little folk of the village were going to Slick and Sharpy for their shoes, and the two brownies worked hard the whole day long. They were pleased.

"Our money-box is getting full," said Slick. "Is it time we did our little trick, Sharpy?"

"It is," said Sharpy. "Now, in future we put a walkaway spell into every pair of shoes. Don't forget!"

Dame Shuffle came that day and ordered a pair of blue boots. "We've got just what you want!" said Slick, showing her a pair. "Try them on!"

She tried them on, and they fitted her so well that she bought them at once, grumbling at the price. "I'll wrap them up for you," said Sharpy, and he took them into the other room to find some paper. He slipped a little yellow powder into each boot and then wrapped them up and took them to Dame Shuffle. Off she went, and wore them out to tea that afternoon.

"Beautiful!" said Mother Nid-Nod, "I'll get a pair from Slick and Sharpy, too."

"So will I," said Mister Tiptap. And the next day off they went to buy a pair each. But on the way they met Dame Shuffle, who looked very worried.

"Someone came in the night and stole my boots," she said. "My beautiful new boots that cost so much. They are quite, quite gone."

"Oh dear – robbers must be about," said Mister Tiptap. "I shall be very careful of mine when I get them."

He got a pair of red shoes and Mother Nid-Nod got a pair of brown shoes with green buckles. Slick and Sharpy grinned at one another when both customers had gone.

"Did you put the walkaway spell in them?" said Slick.

Sharpy nodded. "Yes, both pairs will be back again tonight!" he said. "And we'll put them into our sack ready to take away with us when our money-box is quite full."

That night the spell inside Mother Nid-Nod's brown shoes and Mister Tiptap's red ones began to work. Mother Nid-Nod heard a little shuffling sound and thought it was mice. She called her cat into her bedroom at once.

"Cinders," she said, "catch the mice in this room while I am asleep." So Cinders watched – but instead of mice running about he saw Mother Nid-Nod's shoes walk to the door and all the way downstairs, and hop out of the open kitchen window. How scared he was!

Mister Tiptap's shoes did exactly the same thing. The old man didn't hear anything, he was so sound asleep. But

the brown owl in the woods suddenly saw a pair of red shoes walking along all by themselves, and was so surprised that he almost fell off the branch he was sitting on.

"Who-who-who is that?" he hooted. "Is there someone invisible walking in those shoes? Who-who-who is it?"

But it wasn't anyone, of course. It was just the walkaway spell in the shoes sending them back to the two bad brownies. The people of the village began to get very upset. Everyone who bought lovely new shoes from Slick and Sharpy lost them in the night. And then, when they brought their old shoes to be mended and took them home again, those went too!

Slick and Sharpy just slipped walkaway spells in the mended shoes as well – and, of course, they walked away to the little

toadstool house the very next night!

"Our money-box is full," said Slick. "Most of the shoes we have made for the people here have come back to us – as well as a lot of their old shoes that we mended."

"Good," said Sharpy. "Let's go to another village now. We can settle in and do no work for a long time because we shall have so many pairs of boots and shoes to sell!"

"We'll just make this last pair of high boots for Mister Bigfeet," said Slick. "He has promised us five gold pieces for them – so that means we will have a lot of money from him and if we put the usual walkaway spell in the boots we shall have those, too, because they will come back to us tonight!"

Mister Bigfeet called for the boots that afternoon and paid for them. "I hope no one comes to steal these boots!" he said. "They're beautiful!"

Now, Bigfeet had a little servant called Scurry-About. She was a timid little goblin, very fond of her big master. She thought the boots were lovely, and she polished them till they shone that night.

"Oh, Master!" she said. "I hope no one will steal them!"

"Well, see that they don't!" said Bigfeet and went up to bed. Scurry-About always slept down in the kitchen. The boots were there, too. She looked at them.

"Oh dear – I sleep so very soundly that if anyone comes to steal them I would never hear!" she said. "I know what I'll do! I'll go to sleep wearing them! Then if a robber comes he will have to pull them off my feet and I shall wake up and scream!"

Well, she curled herself up in her small bed with the big boots on her feet. They reached right up to her knees! She fell sound asleep.

And in the night the walkaway spell began to work! The boots wanted to walk back to Slick and Sharpy. But they couldn't, because Scurry-About was wearing them. They began to wriggle and struggle to get themselves off her feet.

She woke up at once. "Who's pulling off the boots? Master, Master, come quickly, someone is stealing your boots!" she cried.

Bigfeet woke up at once and came scrambling down to the kitchen. He was most surprised to find Scurry-About wearing his boots. And dear me, what was this? They leaped off her bed, taking her with them – and then began to walk to the window. Up to the sill they jumped, and then tried to leap out.

But Scurry-About was still in them, and she screamed because she was stuck halfway through the window. "Help, help! The boots are taking me away!"

And then Bigfeet suddenly knew what was happening! "There's a spell in them!" he cried. "A walkaway spell, put there by those tiresome brownies – the rogues! Scurry-About, I'm going to open the window wide and let the boots take you away with them – but I'll follow close behind!"

"Oh, Master! Help me!" squealed poor little Scurry-About, and woke up all the

villagers around, so that they threw on their dressing-gowns and came hurrying to see what was happening.

Bigfeet opened his window wide. The boots set off at top speed with Scurry-About's feet in them, taking her along too. Through the wood and into the lane and down the street – and right up to the front door of Toadstool Cottage went those big top-boots!

And there they kicked at the door to be let in. Scurry-About was crying, and Bigfeet was shouting in rage. All the other villagers were calling out in amazement.

"See! They are walking off to Slick and Sharpy! The wicked brownies! Wait till we get hold of them!"

Slick and Sharpy heard all this and they were very frightened. Slick peeped out of the window. When he saw such an angry crowd he was alarmed.

"Quick, Sharpy," he said. "We must get out of the back door as soon as we can. Don't wait for anything – not even the money-box!"

So they fled down the stairs and opened the back door quietly. Out they went into the night and nobody saw them go.

The top-boots kicked the door down and everyone went inside the house. Scurry-About pulled off the boots, crying.

"They've gone," said Bigfeet, looking all round.

"But they've left behind their money-box full of money – and sacks full of the boots they made for us!" said Mister Tiptap, emptying them out. "Aha! It's our money because we paid it out to them – and they're our boots because they were made for us. How well-off we are!"

Nobody knew where Slick and Sharpy went to, and nobody cared. The villagers kept the boots and shoes and gave little Scurry-About two beautiful pairs for herself.

As for the money, it is being spent on a birthday present for the little Prince of Dreamland, who is five years old next week – he is going to have a box of big wooden soldiers, who march away in rows – and then walk back again! You see, Bigfeet found the walkaway spell in a box at Toadstool Cottage – so won't the little Prince be surprised!

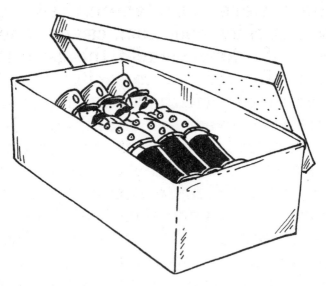

The
Enchanted Goat

Once upon a time a great fair came to the village of Penny-Come-Quick. There were roundabouts, swings, coconut shies, conjurors, clowns, and a score of other splendid things. Little Benny Biggles was so excited that he couldn't sleep for thinking of it all.

He went every single day, and of all the wonderful things at the fair there was one that he simply couldn't take his eyes off. This was a wooden goat with wings on each of its heels.

A Chinaman was in charge of it, and if any one paid fivepence he would make the goat rise into the air, fly round the fairground and then come back again to him. Benny could have watched that all day. He thought it was the most wonderful thing he had ever seen.

"I wonder how it does it?" he said to himself. "Wouldn't I love to ride on it!"

Now no sooner did he think that than his heart began to beat very fast indeed. Why shouldn't he have a ride on the goat?

"I'll just see if I can!" said Benny. So the next day, when the Chinaman was taking fivepences, Benny stood as close to him as he could to see what he did to make the goat fly off.

"It's easy!" said Benny to himself. "Why, he just pulls one ear back, that's all! I could do that myself!"

When the Chinaman's back was turned, and he was telling everyone about his wonderful goat, Benny crept up to it.

"My goat, he will fly all round the fair," said the man. "Give me just one more fivepence and you shall see him go!"

Benny suddenly leaped on the goat's back. All the people cried out "Oh!" in surprise, and the Chinaman turned round quickly. When he saw Benny on his goat, he ran towards him, shouting out something in a strange language that

the boy could not understand.

But before he could get to the goat, Benny pulled back its right ear. In a second the wooden creature rose into the air, all its foot-wings flapping hard. Benny hung on tightly, his breath taken away.

"Ooh!" he cried. "What an adventure! Go on, goat, go on!"

The goat flew right round the fairground, and Benny could see everyone below staring up at him in the greatest astonishment. The people pointed their fingers at him, and shouted to one another.

"See! A little boy is riding the enchanted goat!" they cried.

Benny expected the goat to fly down to the Chinaman after it had gone round the fairground once, for that was what it always did. He thought that the man would be cross with him, but he didn't mind that! He had had the loveliest ride in all his life!

But oh dear me! The goat didn't go down to the Chinaman! After it had circled round the ground once, it suddenly rose much higher in the air and started flying straight towards the setting sun! Benny was too surprised to say anything at first, and then he gave a shout.

"Hi! Stop! You're going the wrong way, goat! Take me back to the fairground! Hurry up and turn round!"

But the goat took no notice of Benny at all. It went on flying towards the sun, very fast and very straight. Benny began to feel frightened. He clung on tightly to the goat's horns, his hair streaming out behind him. Below him he could see fields and hills stretched out very small, like a toy countryside. He saw a train going along a railway line, and it seemed to him to be smaller even than his own clockwork train at home.

"Stop! Stop!" he shouted to the goat. "You are taking me too far! Turn round and go back to the fair!"

Still the goat took no notice. Benny kicked its wooden sides with his feet, but that didn't do any good either. Whatever was he to do?

On and on went the goat, faster than ever. Soon they came to the sea. When they were right over it, the little boy looked downwards. He saw dark blue water stretching out all around him. Soon

no land was in sight at all. Benny had no idea that the sea was so big. He clutched the goat more tightly, afraid that he would fall into the water far below.

The sun sank down into the western sky and darkness came. The stars twinkled brightly, the moon came up, and Benny grew very sleepy. He began to cry, for he was afraid.

"I wish I knew how to stop this goat," he sobbed. "I expect it will go on like this for ever and ever, and I'll go round and round the world till I fall off."

Then he dried his tears and began to think hard.

"If I pull the right ear back to start the goat, perhaps I push it forward to stop it," he thought. But before he did anything, he peeped downwards to see if they were over land or sea. They were still flying over the water, but Benny could see an island not far off. He decided to try and alight on that.

He pushed the goat's right ear forward. Nothing happened at all. The goat still went steadily on. Then the little boy took hold of the left ear, and pulled that back. At once the goat began to slow down!

"I've found the secret, I've found the secret!" cried Benny in delight. "Oh, if only I'd thought of that before!"

He peered below him, and saw that the goat had not quite reached the island, but would land in the water round it. So he quickly pushed the left ear forward again, and pulled the right ear back. The goat at once flew straight onwards. When he was exactly over the island, Benny pushed the right ear forward and pulled the left ear back.

The goat flew down to the land. Benny tried to see what it was like but he could see little, except that he thought he could make out a huge building of some sort. Nearer and nearer to the land came the goat, and at last it was skimming along just above the ground. Then *bump*! It landed, and stood quite still while Benny got off.

The little boy saw that he was at the edge of a wood, but it was so dark that he knew it was no use trying to find anyone to help him. He must wait till the morning. He stretched his stiff legs and yawned for it was long past his bedtime and he was very sleepy.

Then he felt for the goat's ears. He carefully pushed the left ear forward and made certain that the right ear was in its proper position too. Then he found a soft patch of heather and, curling himself up in it, he went fast asleep.

It was day when he awoke, and the sun was shining in the eastern sky. Benny looked around him in surprise, for at first he did not remember how he had arrived there. Then he saw the wooden goat standing near by, and he remembered everything.

"Ooh, I am hungry!" he said, jumping to his feet. "I wonder where I can get something to eat. Then I'll jump on to my old goat and go off home. If I fly to the east, I'm sure to get there sometime. As soon as I see the fairground beneath me, I shall fly down to it!" He looked round him. He could hear the sound of the sea nearby, and he remembered that he was on an island. Behind him was a wood, and to the right was a very high hill – almost a mountain. On the very top was an enormous castle with thousands of glittering windows.

"Good gracious!" said Benny in astonishment. "Whoever lives there?"

He saw a smaller hill nearby, and after carefully hiding the wooden goat under a bush, he started off to go to the top. When he stood on the summit he looked round him. He saw sea on every side, for the island was quite small. It had two hills, the one he was on, and the very high one on which the castle stood. A little wood lay between, and from the very middle of it rose some smoke.

"Someone must live there," said Benny. "I'll go and ask them if they would kindly give me something to eat, for I've never been so hungry in all my life before!"

Down the hill he went, and into the wood. He soon found a little path and

followed it. After a while he came to the strangest house he had ever seen. It was quite small, and was built of precious stones which glittered so brightly that Benny was almost dazzled. Round it was a circle of white stones.

Benny walked up to the circle. He stood outside, trying to see the door of the cottage – but he could see none, though he walked all round it several times.

"Well, I'll just have to go right up and see where it is," said the little boy. So he put his foot over the ring of white stones to walk up to the house.

But good gracious me! He couldn't put it on the ground again! It was held there in the air, though Benny could not see anyone or anything holding it.

Then all at once there came the noise of a hundred trumpets blowing and a thousand bells ringing!

"Oh my! Oh my!" said poor Benny. "This must be a magic circle or something!"

Suddenly there came a voice from the house. Benny looked, and saw a gnome's head peeping out of a window.

"Who are you?" demanded the gnome. "You have put your foot in my magic circle, and started all my bells ringing

and trumpets blowing. Take your foot out."

Benny tried to but he couldn't.

"I can't," he said. "Please undo the spell or whatever it is. I'm getting so tired of standing on one leg. I'm only a little boy coming to ask for something to eat."

"Say your sixteen times table then," said the gnome, sternly.

"Oh, I can't," said Benny, nearly crying. "Why, I'm only up to seven times at school; and I don't know that very well yet."

"Oh, that's all right then," said the gnome, smiling. "I thought you were a wizard or a witch disguised as a little boy. If you had been, you would have known your sixteen times table, but as you don't, I know you are a little boy. I've taken the spell off now. You can come into the magic circle."

Benny's foot was suddenly free. He stepped over the ring of white stones and went up to the glittering house. He looked everywhere for a door, but he couldn't find one.

"Clap your hands twice, and call out 'Open, open' seven times!" said the gnome.

Benny did so, and at once a door appeared in the wall and opened itself in front of him. The gnome looked out and pulled Benny inside by the hand. At once the door disappeared again.

"Why do all these things happen like this?" said Benny, puzzled. "Am I in Fairyland?"

"Not exactly," said the gnome, setting a big bowl of bread and milk in front of Benny. "This island was once part of Fairyland – just the two hills and the wood, you know – and a great giant came and built his castle on the top of the biggest hill."

"I thought giants weren't allowed in Fairyland," said Benny in astonishment.

"They're not," said the gnome, putting a hot cup of cocoa by Benny's side, "but this one was very cunning. He turned himself into a small goblin, and built a tiny castle. Nobody minded, of course, for there are lots of goblins in Fairyland.

But one night he changed himself back to his proper shape, a giant as tall as a house, and made his castle grow big too! What do you think of that?"

"Go on!" said Benny, eating his bread and milk. "This is very exciting!"

"Well, the giant was so big and so powerful that the king and queen couldn't get rid of him," said the gnome. "He was a terrible nuisance, because he would keep capturing fairies and taking them to his castle. Then he would charge the king a thousand pieces of gold to get them back again."

"The horrid monster!" said Benny.

"Then, as they couldn't make the giant go away," said the gnome, "they suddenly thought of putting a spell on the land he owned, and sending it away to the middle of the sea to become an island! So they did that, and off went the two hills and the wood one fine starlit night! They landed in the sea miles away with a terrible splash, and here we are!"

"But how did you come to be here?" asked Benny, puzzled.

"Well, I happened to have built my house in the wood without anyone knowing," said the gnome, sighing. "So, of course, I went too, and I can't get back. The giant was in a terrible temper when he found what had happened. He came tearing down to me, and if I hadn't quickly put a spell round my house, he would certainly have turned me into a hedgehog or something like that."

"And does he live here all alone?" asked Benny.

"No, he has got seven fairies with him," said the gnome. "The king didn't know that he had stolen them on the very night his castle was moved, so of course the poor things are still there. I wish I could rescue them; but there is such a powerful spell all round the castle that I couldn't get near it even if I tried all day!"

"What does he do with the fairies?" asked Benny, finishing his bread and milk to the very last crumb.

287

"They are his servants," said the gnome, "and very hard he makes them work, I can tell you. If they are not quick enough for him, he beats them, and I have often heard them crying, poor things. But they will never be rescued, for no one can get to the castle."

"What a shame!" said Benny. "Oh, how I wish I could rescue them!"

"You're only a little boy," said the gnome scornfully, "you couldn't possibly do anything."

Benny looked at the gnome. Then an idea flashed into his head.

"Tell me, Mister Gnome," he said, "is there a spell on the castle top as well as all around the walls?"

"Of course not!" said the gnome, staring at Benny in surprise. "The castle is much too high for anyone to get on the top. Why do you ask?"

"Because I think I can rescue the fairies!" said Benny, his heart beating very fast. "I've got an enchanted goat here, which I came on, and I believe I could make it fly to the castle roof and, if I could only find the fairies quickly, they could mount on its back and I could take them away with me."

"An enchanted goat!" said the gnome in astonishment. "Then you're not a little boy after all. I'll put a spell on you if you're a witch or a wizard!"

"No, no, don't!" cried Benny. "I really am a little boy. Listen and I'll tell you how I came here."

In a few minutes the gnome knew Benny's story. The little boy took him to where he had hidden the goat, and the gnome grew tremendously excited.

"Oh, Benny!" he cried. "I believe we'll do it! Oh, how grand!"

"Will you come with me?" asked Benny. "I feel a bit frightened all alone."

"Of course I will!" said the gnome. Then he and Benny got on to the goat's

back, Benny pulled the right ear back, and off they went. They flew high above the castle, and then Benny made the goat go downwards.

The castle had a flat roof, and it was quite easy to land there.

"Talk in whispers now," said the gnome. "If the giant hears us, we shall be captured at once. Look! there are some steps going down from the roof. You'd better go down them and see if you can find any of the fairies. I'll wait here."

Benny ran to the steps. He climbed down them very carefully. They went round and round and down and down. At last he came to the end and found himself in a long passage with doors opening off.

"Oh dear! Had I better try each one to see if the fairies are inside?" thought Benny. "No, I won't, I'll go on to those stairs over there, and go down a bit further. If the fairies do the work for the giant, they may be in the kitchen."

He went down some more stairs, and then down some more. They seemed to be

never-ending. At last he heard a
tremendous noise. It came from a room
nearby. The door was open, and Benny
peeped in. He saw an enormous giant
there, lying in the biggest armchair he
had ever seen. He was fast asleep, and
the great noise Benny had heard was
the giant snoring.

"Oh, good!" thought Benny in
delight. "Now I can look about in
safety for the fairies."

He came to a smaller door, and listened.
He thought he could hear the murmur of

little voices behind, and he opened the door. Yes, he was right! Sitting round a big fire, polishing enormous mugs and dishes, was a group of small fairies. One of them was crying.

When the door opened, they all sprang to their feet expecting to see the giant. When they saw Benny, they were so astonished that none of them could speak a word.

"Shh! Shh!" said Benny. "I've come to rescue you! I've got an enchanted goat up on the roof. Hurry up and come along with me. I'll take you back to Fairyland."

The fairies were so full of joy that they ran to Benny and hugged him. Then they ran lightly out of the room and up the stairs, treading very softly indeed when they passed the room where the giant slept. Benny followed them, and at last they all reached the roof. The gnome stood there with the goat, and greeted them in delight.

How they hugged one another and smiled for joy! Two of the fairies wept for gladness and Benny had to lend them

his handkerchief to dry their eyes.

"Come on," said the gnome, at last. "We mustn't stop here. If the giant wakes he will be sure to miss you and put a spell on you somehow. Are you all here?"

Benny counted the fairies.

"Good gracious!" he said in dismay. "There are only six of them! Didn't you say there were seven, Mister Gnome?"

"Oh, where's Tiptoe, where's Tiptoe?" cried all the other fairies. "We've left her behind! She was watering the plants in the greenhouse, and we've left her behind!"

"Well, call her," said the gnome. "If the giant wakes it can't be helped. I expect she will get up here before he knows there is anything the matter."

So all together the fairies called her:

"Tiptoe! Tiptoe! Come up to the roof at once! Tiptoe!"

A little voice from far below answered them. "I'm coming!"

Then suddenly there came a thunderous roar. The giant had woken up!

"WHO'S THAT CALLING!" he shouted. "YOU'VE WAKENED ME FROM MY SLEEP, YOU WICKED FAIRIES! I'LL PUNISH YOU, I WILL!"

"Ooh!" said the fairies, turning pale.

"It's all right," said the gnome. "By the time he's looked into the kitchen and called for you a few times, we shall be gone! Look, here's Tiptoe!"

The seventh fairy came running up the steps to the roof. In a second the others explained everything to her.

"Get on the goat," said the gnome, "the giant is getting very angry indeed."

The fairies began to clamber on the goat – but whatever do you think! There was only room for five of them! The goat was much too small.

"Oh my, oh my!" groaned the gnome. "I

don't think I've time to make it big enough for us all, but I'll try. Stand away everyone."

He drew a chalk ring round the goat, clapped his hands, and began to dance round and round it, singing a magic song. Little by little the wooden creature grew bigger.

The giant below was roaring more angrily than ever and then Benny suddenly heard his footsteps coming up the stairs! "Quick, he's coming!" he shouted. The gnome hastily rubbed out the chalk circle with his foot and ran to the goat. He pushed Benny on first and then he helped all the fairies on. Last of all he got on himself, though there was really hardly room for him. Just as they were all on, the giant appeared at the opening to the roof.

Benny pulled back the right ear of the goat and at once the animal rose into the air. The giant gave a tremendous roar of anger and surprise, and fell down the steps in astonishment. By the time he had picked himself up,

and was ready to work a powerful spell on the goat to bring it back, it was far away in the sky.

Benny was trembling with excitement, and so were all the others. For a long while no one spoke. Then the fairies all began to talk at once, and thanked Benny and the gnome over and over again for rescuing them. Benny listened to their little high voices, and thought them the sweetest sound he had ever heard.

After a long time he looked below him. To his great astonishment he saw that he was flying just over his own home! Away to the right was the fairground, and the music of the roundabouts came faintly to Benny's ears.

"Oh, I think I'll go down here," said Benny. "There's my home, and I would like to see my mother and tell her I'm all right. Do you mind if I get off here? The gnome will take you safely back to Fairyland."

So down they all went, and Benny jumped off the goat at the end of his own garden.

"Goodbye," he said. "And would you mind sending the goat back to the Chinaman at the fair! I expect he will be upset not to have it."

"Certainly," said the gnome, "we can easily do that. Well, thank you for all your help, Benny. Goodbye!"

"Goodbye, goodbye!" called the fairies, as the goat once more rose into the air. Benny watched them until he could no longer see them, and then ran indoors to tell his mother all his adventures.

"I must go to the fair tomorrow to see if the fairies have sent the goat back," said Benny. And the next day off he went. Sure enough, the goat was there – but will you believe it, the gnome had forgotten to make it small again, and it was simply enormous!

The Chinaman was so astonished! He couldn't make it out at all.

"It is a very strange thing!" he said, over and over again. "Who can tell me what has happened?"

Benny told him – but he needn't have bothered, for the Chinaman didn't believe a word of his story! He took his enchanted goat away after the fair was over, and, as far as I know, nobody has ever heard of him since.

The Lost
Doll's Pram

"Mummy, I do so wish Tibbles wouldn't keep jumping into my doll's pram," said Ellie. "How can I stop her?"

"Well, you could stop her by doing what I used to do, when you were a baby in your pram," said her mother. "You can put a net over the pram so that no cat can jump into it."

"Oh dear – I don't want to do that," said Ellie. "It would be an awful bother to have to do that every time I put my dolls to sleep. I shall shout at Tibbles next time I find her in my doll's pram!"

Ellie found her there the very next morning, curled up under the eiderdown, fast asleep. Didn't Ellie shout! Tibbles gave a miaow of surprise, and leaped out of the pram at once. She was never shouted at by Ellie and she didn't like it at all.

"You are not to get into the pram," said Ellie to Tibbles. "I have told you ever so often. You are a naughty little cat. Do you want to smother Rosebud or Josephine by lying on top of them? Shoo! Go away!"

Tibbles ran away – but will you believe it, as soon as Ellie went indoors again, Tibbles jumped right into the pram once more!

She did love that pram. It was so soft inside and so cosy. She loved cuddling down, curling herself up and going to sleep in peace and quiet there.

"It just fits me nicely," she thought. "I can share it with the dolls. They never seem to mind. They don't even kick me."

Now the next day three naughty boys came along with a naughty little girl. They saw some apples hanging on the trees in Ellie's garden, and they crept in at the gate to take some.

Ellie saw them from the window. She rushed out into the garden. "You bad children! That's stealing! Go away and leave my daddy's apples alone."

"Give us some!" shouted the biggest boy.

"No, certainly not. If you had come to ask my daddy properly, he would have given you a basketful," cried Ellie. "But people who steal don't get any. Go away!"

"You're a horrid little girl!" shouted the boy. "We'll pay you back!"

And then Ellie's mother came out and the four naughty children ran away. They came peeping over the wall again the day after – but not to take the apples. They meant to pay Ellie back for sending them away.

"Look – there's her doll's pram," whispered the little girl. "Let's take it away into the park and hide it where she can't find it. That will teach her to shout at us and send us away. Quick, Billy – there's no one about – you slip in and get it."

Billy opened the back gate, ran into the garden and took hold of the pram handle. He wheeled the little pram at top speed out of the gate. *Slam!* The gate shut and the four children hurried down the lane to the park.

"She hasn't got any dolls in the pram," said the little girl. "I'd have thrown them into the bushes if she had!"

What a very horrid little girl she was! She had dolls of her own and loved them – and yet she would have done an unkind thing to someone else's dolls! Well, well – some people are strange, aren't they?

The boys stuffed the pram into the middle of a big bush and left it there.

Then they went back to Ellie's garden to see what she said when she came out and found her pram missing.

She soon came out with her two dolls, meaning to take them for a walk, as she always did each morning. But where was her pram? It was nowhere to be seen! Ellie looked everywhere for it and then she saw the four heads of the giggling children, peeping over the wall.

"Have you seen my pram?" she called.

"Yes," they called back.

"Where is it?" shouted Ellie.

"It's hidden in the park where you can't find it!" called the biggest boy. "Ha, ha! You'll never find it again!"

"Mummy, Mummy, come here!" called Ellie, almost in tears. But her mother had just gone next door and she didn't come. So Ellie had to make up her mind herself what she was going to do.

"I must go and look in the park," she thought. "Oh, dear – suppose it rains? My lovely pram will be soaked. Suppose I don't find it? How am I to know where those bad children have put it?"

305

She put her dolls down just inside the house, ran down the garden again, into the lane and was soon in the park. Now where should she look?

She hunted here and she hunted there. She looked in this bush and that, but she couldn't find her pram.

"Oh dear – there are such a lot of bushes and trees!" thought poor Ellie. "I could look all day long and never find my pram. Where can it be?"

It was very well hidden indeed. Someone else was well hidden there too. And that was Tibbles!

Tibbles had been in the pram when the bad children had run off with it, curled up as usual under the eiderdown, fast asleep. When the children had taken the pram, Tibbles had thought it was Ellie taking the dolls for a walk. She hadn't dared to pop her head up, in case Ellie was cross with her. So she just lay there, wondering why the pram went so fast that morning. Then suddenly it was pushed into the bushes, and was still. Tibbles shut her eyes and went to sleep again.

She woke up after a time and stretched herself. Everything seemed very quiet. Tibbles felt hungry and thought she would jump out of the pram and go and find her dinner. She had forgotten that the pram had been taken for a walk – she thought she was still in garden!

She poked her head out from under the covers and looked round. What was this? She was somewhere quite strange! This wasn't her garden. Tibbles sat right up, very frightened.

Where was she? Where was Ellie?

What had happened? And dear me, was this rain beginning to fall?

It was. Big drops pattered down on Tibbles, and she crouched down. She hated the rain. She suddenly felt very lonely and frightened and she gave a loud miaow.

"MIAOW! MEE-OW-EE-OW-EE-OW-EE-OW!"

Nothing happened except that the rain pattered down more loudly. One enormous drop fell splash! on to Tibbles' nose, and she miaowed angrily.

The rain made a loud noise on the bracken around, and Tibbles couldn't think what it was. She didn't dare to jump out of the pram.

"MIAOW-OW-OW!" she wailed, at the top of her voice.

Ellie was not very far off, and she heard this last miaow. She stopped. That sounded like a cat's voice! Was there a cat lost in the park, caught in the rain that was now pouring down? Poor thing!

"MEEEEEEEEE-OOOW-OOOOW!"

wailed Tibbles, and Ellie hurried towards the sound. "MEEE-OW!"

"It seems to come from that bush over there," thought the little girl, and went to it. Another loud wail came from the spot.

"Meee-ow-ow-ow! MEE-ow-ow-OW!"

And then Ellie suddenly saw the handle of her pram sticking out of the bush. How delighted she was! She ran to it and gave the handle a tug – out came her doll's pram – and there, sitting in the middle of it, scared and lonely, was Tibbles!

"Oh, Tibbles! It was you I heard miaowing!" cried Ellie, in surprise. "You must have been asleep in the pram again when those children ran off with it. Oh, Tibbles, I am glad you were in it – it was your miaowing that made me find it! I'll never scold you again for getting into the pram!"

She put up the hood and drew the waterproof cover over Tibbles so that the frightened cat shouldn't get soaked. And then off she went home with her precious pram, not minding the rain in the least because she was so pleased to have found her pram again.

Tibbles couldn't imagine why Ellie made such a fuss of her, but she liked it all the same. The funny thing was that she never, never got into the doll's pram again. She was so afraid it would run off with her into the park and lose her!

So do you know what she does? She gets into the doll's cot up in the playroom and goes to sleep there! I've seen her, and she really does look sweet, curled up with her tail round her nose.

Tommy's White Duck

Tommy had a real live duck of his own. He had had it given to him when it was just a little yellow duckling, and somehow or other nobody had ever thought what it would be like when it grew up!

At first it was just a dear little yellow bird, crying "Peep peep, peep!" all day. Tommy's father made it a tiny run of its own, with wire netting all round, and a small coop for it to sleep in. Tommy fed it and gave it a small bowl of water to swim in.

And then, quite suddenly, it seemed, it began to grow! By the time the middle of the summer came it was quite a big duck. It had lost its pretty yellow down and grew snowy-white feathers. It no longer said "Peep,

peep!" but quacked quite loudly.

Father had to make the run bigger.
The days went on, and the duck grew
and grew. It could no longer swim in
the bowl, nor even in the tin bath
which Mother put out for it.

"Daddy, could we make a little pond
for my duck to swim in?" asked
Tommy one day. "I could help you dig it
out, couldn't I?"

"Dear me, I'm not going to dig a
pond for that noisy old duck!" said his
father. "It's got too big for us now,
Tommy. We shall have to sell it."

"Daddy!" cried Tommy, his eyes full

of tears. "Sell my duck! Oh, I couldn't! Why, perhaps somebody would have it for their dinner – it would be simply dreadful!"

"Well, Tommy, it's really too big now," said his father. "Besides, it has such a noisy quack."

"But, Daddy, if we made it a little pond of its own, it would be happy and wouldn't quack so much," said Tommy. "I'm sure that's why it's quacking such a lot – because it wants a swim."

"Well, then, what about letting the farmer's wife have the duck back?" asked Father. "She gave it to you when it was a duckling, and maybe she'd like it back now, to go with her other ducks. Then it could swim on her big pond."

Tommy didn't say any more. He could see that his father didn't want the duck, and that it would have to go. But he was very sad about it, and he went to the garden to talk to the duck.

"Quack!" said the duck joyfully when it saw Tommy.

"Hello," said Tommy. "Dear old duck,

I'm afraid you're going to be given away, and won't live with me any more."

"Quack!" said the duck, and gave Tommy a small, loving peck.

Well, the very next day the duck was taken down the lane to the farm, and Tommy had to say goodbye to it. The duck seemed very puzzled, but when it saw the other ducks it went quite mad with joy and dashed into the pond, waddling so fast that it fell over its own big flat feet!

"There you are!" said Father, turning to Tommy. "See how pleased the duck is to be here!"

"But it will miss me when it's got used to being here," said Tommy. "It will want me, Daddy."

"Nonsense!" said his father, laughing, and he took Tommy home.

Well, it so happened that Tommy was right, for the very next day the duck had a look round and thought, "Where's Tommy? Where's my own run? Where's the garden I know so well? Where, oh where, is Tommy?"

314

The duck sat in the sun and thought. It loved Tommy and wanted to be with him. So what did it do but walk over the farmyard and squeeze under the gate, and set off waddling up the lane, back to Tommy's house and garden!

"Quack!" it said as it went. "Quack!" Up the dusty lane it went, and at last it came to Tommy's house. Nobody was in. Tommy was at school. Tommy's father was at work. Tommy's mother had slipped in the house next door to talk to Mrs White. But the baby was in her pram in the garden fast asleep.

"Quack!" said the duck, squeezing through the hedge and looking round

for Tommy. But just then something happened. There came the sound of thundering hoofs and two of the farm-horses galloped up the lane!

Someone had left the field gate open, and the horses had got out. They were excited and were running after one another. And what do you think happened? Why, one of them saw the garden gate open and galloped through into the garden!

The duck knew quite well this was wrong. Suppose the horse knocked the pram over? Good gracious, look at the mess it was making of the lovely lawn, sinking its hard hoofs deep into the grass!

There was only one thing to do, and the duck knew what it was! It knew quite well that usually when it quacked loudly, Tommy's mother came to the window and said, "Shh! Shh! You'll wake the baby!" And if only the duck could make her come, she would see the galloping horse and everything would be put right! The duck didn't know that

Tommy's mother was not in the house, of course.

It began to quack. How it quacked! You should have heard it! "Quack quack, quack, quack, QUACK, QUACK, QUACK!"

Tommy's mother heard the loud quacking from the next-door house. "Well!" she said in surprise. "That sounds just like our duck – but it can't be, because Tommy and his father took it down to the farm yesterday."

"Quack, quack, quack, quack, quack, QUACK, QUACK!" cried the duck, as the horse galloped round the garden once more.

"It must be our duck!" said Tommy's mother and she ran back home to see – and, of course, she at once saw the horse in the garden!

"Oh! Oh!" she cried. "It will knock the pram over! It will knock the pram over!"

She caught up a stick and ran to the excited horse. She drove it to the gate – and it went out at a gallop, off down the lane to the farm, where the other horse had also gone.

Mother shut the gate. She was quite pale and frightened. Tommy came running home from school and wondered what was the matter.

"Oh, Tommy!" said Mother. "One of those great farm-horses got into the garden this afternoon when I was next door, and nearly knocked the pram over!"

"But how did you know it was here, galloping about?" asked Tommy. "Did you hear Baby crying?"

"No – I heard your old duck quacking!" said his mother. "Fancy that, Tommy! It must have walked all the way up the lane to get back to you and it quacked loudly when it saw the horse, and warned me."

"Oh, you good old duck!" cried Tommy, running to his duck and putting his arms round its snowy neck.

"You good old thing! You saved Baby! Oh, Mum – I do wish we could keep my duck! Look how it's come all the way home again!"

"You shall keep it," said Mother, and she patted the surprised duck on the head. "When I tell Daddy about how it warned me this afternoon by quacking so loudly, he will be sure to say it can stay with you now."

So Tommy's mother told his father – and what do you think he and Tommy are doing this week? Guess!

Yes – they are both digging out a nice little pond for the duck, for it is to stay with Tommy, of course. Won't it be pleased to have a pond of its own! Yesterday it laid its first egg – and Father had it for breakfast!

"Quack!" said the duck. "I'm one of the family. You can't get rid of me! Quack!"

The
Sensible Train

Fiona-Mary is very puzzled. You see, something very surprising happened, and she doesn't know whether it was a dream or whether it was real. I must tell you, and see what you think.

Well, the toys in the playroom were always up to tricks every night. The teddy bear built towers with the bricks and knocked them down over the rabbit whenever he came by. The sailor-doll rolled the ball at the toy soldier and knocked him over every time. The white dog shut the black dog's tail in the cupboard door and made him yell.

That was the sort of thing they did. But one night they got a shock.

They all got up on to the table to watch the two goldfish swimming in their bowl. The goldfish didn't like the toys at all, because the toys used to press their noses against the outside of the bowl and make rude faces at the goldfish. This was really very frightening indeed.

Now the yellow-haired doll wanted to see in at the top of the bowl, so she stood up and looked in. She was wearing a pretty bead necklace that had come out of a Christmas cracker – and just as she leaned over the water, this necklace broke!

All the beads fell into the water! How upset the doll was! She began to cry and squeal, and all the toys wanted to know what was the matter.

The teddy bear immediately said he would get the beads for the yellow-haired doll. He leaned over the bowl and put in a long arm, meaning to scoop up the beads from the bottom. But one of the goldfish swam at his paw and tried to bite it. The teddy bear gave a yell and fell head-first into the water!

There he stuck, head in the bowl and legs waving wildly in the air.

"Pull him out, pull him out!" cried the rabbit. But when the toys tried to do this, the bowl half tipped over, and the toys knew that they would spill water and fish if they pulled any harder.

They were frightened and climbed down quickly from the table.

"What shall we do, what shall we do, what shall we do?" they kept saying. But they did nothing at all, while the poor teddy bear was half drowning in the goldfish bowl, and the fish were nibbling at his ears.

Now the railway train, who hadn't been able to climb up on to the table, was very upset when he heard about the teddy bear. He liked the teddy bear, who often drove him round the playroom at night.

"We must do something!" cried the train, clanking all his carriages. "Quick! Quick!"

But nobody could think what to do. Then the train, who was very sensible, gave a loud whistle and said, "Well, if you can't do something, Fiona-Mary will! I'm off to tell her!" And before the toys could stop him, he had unhitched his carriages and rushed out of the room, across the passage, and into Fiona-Mary's bedroom!

And this is where Fiona-Mary comes into the story. She woke up, of course, for no one can sleep with a clockwork train rushing round and round the room,

whistling loudly. As soon as she sat up, the train rushed out of the bedroom, across the passage, and back to the playroom. It knew very well that Fiona-Mary would follow it in surprise!

She did. She jumped out of bed and ran in astonishment to the playroom.

"Train! Did you really come into my bedroom?" she asked. "Who wound you up? Who . . . ?"

And then she saw the poor teddy bear still struggling in the bowl of water! She ran to the table at once and jerked him out. He gasped and spluttered, and couldn't say a word.

She squeezed the water from his fur and rubbed him with a towel to dry him. "Whatever do you want to go and swim in the goldfish bowl for?" she said. "What a silly you are!"

All the toys sat quite still and didn't say a word. Even the train had run into a corner and was quite still too. They were afraid of waking the grown-ups. Fiona-Mary yawned, rubbed her eyes, and went back to bed.

In the morning she awoke and remembered what had happened. "But it couldn't have happened!" she said. "It was just a dream. I know it was!"

And she was quite, quite sure it was. But the funny thing is – the teddy bear's fur was still damp, and the yellow-haired doll's beads were in the goldfish bowl! Now what do you think of that? Fiona-Mary simply doesn't know what to believe!

The Little
Prickly Family

Once upon a time all the animals in Fir
Tree Wood lived together in peace and
happiness. There were the rabbits and
the toads, the hedgehogs and the mice,
the squirrels and the moles, and many
others.

Then one day King Loppy, the sandy
rabbit, sat down on what he thought
was a brown heap of leaves – but it was
Mr Prickles the hedgehog. He didn't
like being sat on, and he stuck all his
sharp spines upright, so that King
Loppy jumped up with a shout of pain.

"How dare you prick the King of the
Wood?" cried Loppy, standing his ears
up straight in his anger. "You did it on
purpose!"

"No, I didn't," said Mr Prickles,
"really I didn't. But it's not nice to be

sat on quite so hard."

"Well, I banish you from the wood!" said King Loppy, and he pointed with his paw towards the east, where the wood grew thinner. "Go away at once, and take your horrid prickly family with you."

Mr Prickles could do nothing else but obey. So sadly he went to fetch his wife and his six prickly children. They packed up all they owned, and walked out of Fir Tree Wood.

Now they hadn't been gone long when a family of red goblins came to the wood. They went to the Bluebell Dell, which was a pretty little hollow, and made their home there, right in the very middle of the wood.

At first the creatures of the wood took no notice, but soon the goblins made their lives so miserable that even King Loppy vowed he would turn the goblins out.

But he couldn't! The goblins knew too much magic, and the animals were always afraid to say what they really thought for fear of being turned into mushrooms or earwigs. So they had to put up with their larders being raided each night, their firewood stolen, and their young ones frightened by the dreadful noises and ugly faces that the goblins made.

Once every month, when the moon was full, the goblins did a strange, barefoot dance in the dell. They danced round and round in the moonlight, holding hands and singing loud songs.

All the animals were kept awake, and didn't they grumble – but not very loud, in case the red goblins heard and punished them.

"If anyone can get rid of these ugly red creatures for me, he shall be king instead of me!" declared Loppy one night. "Our lives are a misery now, and these goblins must go!"

Well, a good many of the animals thought they would like to be king and wear the woodland crown, but try as they would, they couldn't think of a plan to make the goblins go.

Frisky the red squirrel wrote them a polite letter, and begged them to leave, but the only reply he had was to see all his nuts stolen one bright moonlight night.

Then Mowdie the mole wrote a very stern letter, and said that she would get a policeman from the world of humans, and have them all locked up, if they didn't go away, but they came and laughed so loudly at her that she shivered with fright and didn't go out shopping for three days.

Then bold Mr Hare marched right up to the goblins one day and ordered them out of the wood. He took a whip with him, and threatened to beat each goblin if they didn't obey him.

The goblins sat round and smiled. When Mr Hare tried to use his whip he found that he couldn't move! The goblins had used magic, and he was stuck fast to the ground! Then they tied him up to a birch-tree all night long. Loppy found him the next morning, and Mr Hare vowed that he would never go near those horrid red goblins again!

After that no one did anything, till one day a letter came to Loppy from Mr Prickles the hedgehog. He opened it; and this is what it said:

Dear Your Majesty,

I think I can get rid of the goblins for you, but I do not want to be king. I only want to be allowed to come and live in Fir Tree Wood with all my friends once more. Please let me.

Your loving servant,
Prickles

When Loppy had read the letter he sat down and wrote an answer. This is what he said:

Dear Mr Prickles,
   You may come back here to live if you can get rid of the goblins. But I don't believe you can.
                    Your loving king,
                    Loppy

When Mr Prickles got the letter he was overjoyed, for he felt certain he could get rid of the goblins. He looked up his calendar, and found that the next full-moon night was three nights ahead. On that night the red goblins would have their barefoot dance.

That day Mr Prickles went to see Tibbles the pixie, who was a great friend of his.

"I want you to do something for me," he said. "Will you go to the red goblins in Fir Tree Wood and tell them that someone has sent you to warn them against the magic pins and needles?"

"Goodness!" said Tibbles, with a laugh. "What a funny message – and whatever are the pins and needles?"

"Never mind about that," said Mr Prickles. "You just go and give that message, there's a good pixie, and you can come back and have tea with us."

So Tibbles set off to Bluebell Dell, and when he saw the red goblins he gave them the message.

"Someone has sent me to give you a warning," he said, in a very solemn voice. "You are to beware of the magic pins and needles."

"Ooh!" said the goblins, looking scared. "What are they? And what will they do? And who told you to warn us?"

"I can answer no questions," said Tibbles, and he walked off, leaving the goblins wondering whatever the message meant.

Now, when the night of the full moon came, Mr Prickles and his wife and family made their way to Bluebell Dell. The red goblins were already beginning their barefoot dance. Their shoes and stockings were laid in a neat pile under a tree.

Without being seen, Mrs Prickles went to the pile, picked them up, and took them to the lily-pond not far off. She dropped all the shoes and stockings into the water, and then went back to her family.

"Are you all ready?" whispered Mr Prickles. "Then – *roll!*"

With one accord all the hedgehogs curled themselves up tightly into balls, and rolled down the dell to the bottom where the goblins were busy dancing. They rolled all among their feet, and soon there was a terrible shouting and crying.

336

"Ooh! Ooh! I've trodden on a thorn! I've trodden on a prickle! Ooh! What's this!"

The hedgehogs rolled themselves in and out, and the goblins couldn't help treading on them. The prickles

ran into their bare feet, and they hopped about in pain.

"What is it? What is it?" they cried; but at that moment the moon went in, and the goblins couldn't see anything. They just went on treading on the prickly hedgehogs, and cried out in pain and fright.

Then the head goblin suddenly gave a cry of dismay, "It must be the magic pins and needles! It must be! We were warned against them, we were told to beware! Quick, put on your shoes and stockings before we get into their power!"

But the goblins couldn't find their pile of shoes and stockings – and no wonder, for they were all down at the bottom of the pond. They ran here and there looking for them, and Mr Hedgehog and his family rolled here and there after them. How those hedgehogs enjoyed themselves!

"The pins and needles have taken our shoes!" cried the goblins. "Oh, oh, what shall we do? The pins and needles have found us!"

"Quick!" cried the head goblin. "We must go back to Goblin Town and buy some more shoes for our feet. We must never come back here again!"

Off the goblins ran, as fast as they could, and the hedgehogs rolled after them. If any goblin stopped to take breath he at once felt a prickly something on his foot, and he gave a cry of fright and ran on.

They made such a noise that all the animals in the wood came out to see what was the matter; and just then the moon shone out. The surprised animals saw the red goblins running for their lives, with the whole of the little prickly family of hedgehogs after them!

When the goblins were really gone, everyone crowded round the hedgehogs.

"You brave things to chase away those goblins!" cried Loppy the king. "How could you dare to do such a thing! You are very plucky, Mr Prickles."

"He shall be king!" shouted the animals.

"No," said Mr Prickles, modestly. "I am not great enough to be king. Loppy is far better than I am; but, please, Your Majesty, may I come back to live here, with all my prickly family?"

"Of course!" Loppy said gladly. "But do tell me – how did you manage to chase the goblins away, Mr Prickles?"

"That is a secret," said the hedgehog, and he wouldn't say another word.

340

Then he and all his prickly family came back to their home in the wood again and were very happy. Everyone praised them, and King Loppy had them to tea once a week, so you see he had quite forgiven Mr Prickles for having pricked him when he sat down upon him.

As for the red goblins, they were never heard of again, but folk do say that whenever they think of that last moonlight night in Fir Tree Wood they get a funny feeling in their feet, and then they say:

"Ooh, I've got pins and needles!"

Have you ever felt that way too?

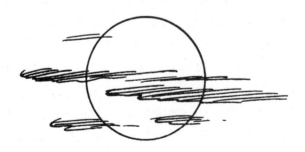

The Dog With
the Very Long Tail

There was once a dog with a very long tail. His name was Ginger, because he was just the colour of ginger, and he belonged to little Terry Brown.

Terry was fond of Ginger. He went about everywhere with his dog, and played games with him when he came out of school. Ginger loved Terry too, and would have done anything in the world for him. His tail never stopped wagging when he was with Terry.

One day Terry was very excited. There was to be a grand garden party in the Rectory garden, with sweet-stalls, competitions, baby shows and dog shows. Terry was going, and he made up his mind to buy some peppermint sweets and to have a bottle of ginger beer and two dips in the bran-tub.

"There's to be a maypole dance too," he told his mother, "and I shall watch that. Mr Jones is having a coconut shy, and I shall have two tries at that."

"Well, I will give you two pounds to spend," said his mother. "That should be plenty for everything, Terry."

"Oh, thank you," said Terry. "I shall take Ginger with me and buy him a bar of chocolate. He'll love that."

When the day came Terry and Ginger walked to the garden party. Terry had

a two pound coin in his pocket, and he was planning all he would do with it. He looked round the grounds and decided that he would start with a go at the coconut shy. He thought it would be lovely to win a big nut.

"I'll have a go," he said to the man. "How much?"

"Three balls for ten pence," said the man. Terry put his hand into his pocket to get his money – and, oh dear me – it was gone! There was a hole at the bottom and the coin had dropped out!

Terry was so upset. He went back to look for his money but he couldn't find it anywhere. Ginger went with him and was just as upset as his master.

"Now I can't buy any sweets or ginger beer, or have any dips in the bran-tub," said poor Terry, sadly. "All my money is gone. Oh, Ginger, I do think it's bad luck, don't you?"

Ginger pushed his nose into Terry's hand and looked up at him with big brown eyes. He was very sorry for his master. He thought he would go and look for the lost money by himself, so he trotted off, nose to ground, trying to find the coin.

Suddenly Ginger came to where a great many dogs were all gathered together with their masters and mistresses, and he ran up to a collie dog called Rover, a great friend of his.

"What are you all doing here?" he asked Rover.

"Waiting for the dog shows," answered Rover.

"I hope you win a prize," said Ginger.

345

"Aren't you going in for the show?" asked Rover.

"No," said Ginger, wagging his tail. "My little master, Terry, is very sad. He has just lost all his money and I'm looking for it."

Just at that moment the dog show began, and the dogs moved into the ring. Ginger stayed to watch. It was a comic dog show, and there were prizes for the fattest dog, the thinnest dog, the dog with the saddest eyes, and the dog with the shortest legs. Ginger thought it was very funny.

"Now then!" cried the man who was running the dog show. "Which dog has the longest tail! Come along, everybody! I've got a measuring tape here to measure the tails with! Bring in your dogs! The one with the longest tail gets two pounds!"

Now when Ginger heard that, a good idea suddenly came into his head! Surely no dog had a longer tail than his! Everybody laughed at his tail because it was so very long. He would trot into the ring and show it to the judge!

So Ginger pushed his way through the people watching and trotted into the ring, where other dogs stood having their tails measured.

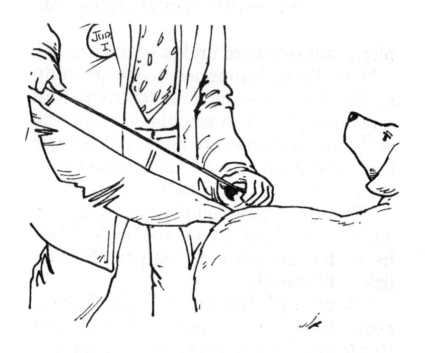

Ginger went right up to the judge
and stuck his tail out to be measured.

"Ha!" cried the judge. "Here is a dog
who thinks his tail is quite the longest!
Stand still, dog, and let me measure it!"

All the people laughed and Ginger
stood quite still while the judge
measured his tail.

"My goodness, what a long one!" he
cried. "Why, it's half a metre long! Little
dog, I think you must have the prize!
Who is the owner of this dog? Will he

please step forward and take the prize?"

Now Terry happened to be peeping at the dog show at that moment and most astonished to see his dog. He was still more surprised to hear that Ginger had won a prize, and he stepped into the ring to take it for him.

"Two pounds!" said the judge, and he gave a nice bright coin to Terry. Then he patted Ginger and the grateful dog licked his hand.

"Good old Ginger!" said Terry, running off with him. "Fancy you thinking of putting yourself in for the longest-tailed dog! I know why you did it, Ginger! You did it because you were sorry that I had lost my money! You're the cleverest, dearest dog in the world, and I'm going to buy you a bun, two biscuits and a bar of chocolate!"

Ginger wagged his long tail and barked for joy. He bounded along by Terry and when his little master had bought him all that he had said he would, he wagged his long tail quite two hundred times a minute.

"Wuff, wuff!" he said, and he ate up the bun, the biscuits, and the chocolate in one gulp!

"Good old Ginger," said Terry. "Now come along to the coconut shy! I'll see if I can't get a coconut this time!"

Off they went – and Terry knocked down the largest coconut of the lot! Wasn't he lucky? Then he went to buy some sweets and some ginger beer, and had three dips in the bran-tub – all with Ginger's two pounds; and you may be sure there wasn't a prouder dog than Ginger at the garden party that day!

What a Surprise!

Barry was very fond of birds, and every morning he put out crumbs for them, and a saucer of fresh water. He made a bird-table, too – just a piece of wood on the top of a pole – and from it he hung strings of unshelled peanuts which he had carefully threaded together, and a coconut with a hole made at each end. He put all kinds of tit-bits on the table, and you should have seen the birds that came to visit it!

When Barry's birthday came, the postman knocked at the door and left three parcels, a small one and two big ones. Inside the small one was a silver pencil – and inside the two big ones were wooden nesting-boxes to put up in the garden for the birds to nest in! Barry was so pleased.

"Just what I've always wanted!" he said, looking at the two boxes in delight. They were very nicely made, and the top part, which made a slanting roof, could be lifted up – so that Barry would be able to peep inside and see if any bird had begun to nest there.

"I shall put these nesting-boxes up today," said the little boy. "I shall put one in the chestnut tree – I know a fine place there – and one I shall fasten among the rose ramblers. There is such a small hole in each for the birds to get in and out that I am sure only the tiny tits will make their homes there. What fun it will be!"

So out he went very happily into the garden, and soon the two nesting-boxes were in their places. One was well hidden among the ramblers and the other was neatly hung on the trunk of a small chestnut tree, protected by an overhanging branch.

"If I were you, Barry," said his mother, "I would hang up bits of fat or

peanuts near your new nesting-boxes, and then, when the tits come to them, they will see the boxes and perhaps think they are good nesting-places."

So Barry hung a few peanuts by each box, and begged a piece of suet to hang up too. In ten minutes' time the tits had found the nuts and the suet, and were very busily pecking away at them. Barry could hear them calling to one another in excitement.

"This is suet, this is, this is suet, this is! Peanuts, peanuts, peanuts! This is suet!"

The tits were pleased to find more food in the garden. They thought that Barry was the nicest, kindest boy in the world, and they were always happy in his garden. One of them flew to the top of a nesting-box. He wondered what it was – it hadn't been there before. He hopped about all over it, sometimes the right way up, sometimes upside down. He didn't really mind whether he swung one way or another!

Then he called to his wife, "Come and see!"

She flew down to him. "Look!" said the tit in excitement. "There is a little hole here. It leads into a nice dark room. Let us go inside and see whether it would be a good place to nest in."

So in they went, and they both decided that it would be exactly right. This was the box that Barry had put in the rose ramblers. The other box was taken by another pair of excited tits, who were most delighted to find such a fine nesting-place.

"It's near plenty of food!" they sang. "It's in the garden of the nicest boy in the world! There are no cats! We shall be safe, safe, safe!"

Then they began to build their cosy nests. They made them of the softest things they could find – bits of moss taken from the ditch, a great many hairs from the post against which the brown horses in the field rubbed themselves each day. And some hairs from the dog next door. When he shook himself a few hairs flew from his coat, and the tits were always on the watch

for these. They would hunt about the lawn for them.

Then they lined their nests with soft feathers. Some they found in the hen-run, and how they squabbled with the sparrows over them! The sparrows liked the feathers too, to make a lining for their nests, and tried their best to take them all – but the tits pounced down in a flash, and carried off most of the downy feathers under the very beaks of the angry sparrows!

The nest of the tits in the rose rambler box was finished first. It was so cosy and warm. Barry knew that they were building there, for he watched them carrying moss and hair in their beaks to the ramblers. He was delighted. One day, when he knew that both the tits had left the nest, he went quietly to it and lifted up the roof-lid. He gazed inside before he shut down the lid, and to his great delight saw five pretty little eggs. Now there would be crowds of fluffy yellow baby tits calling all over the garden to their parents!

He ran indoors to tell his mother.

"I'm so glad," she said. "But if I were you, Barry, I wouldn't peep inside any more. The tits may not like it, and it would be so dreadful if you made them desert their nest and leave their eggs or young ones. It does sometimes happen, you know."

357

So Barry did not go and peep any more. When he did the next time he got a great surprise, as you will hear.

Now, as you probably know, all birds and animals can see the little folk, although very few humans can do so. The tits especially are friendly with them, for the fairies love the merry, pretty little birds, with their bright voices and amusing ways.

Very often the tits went to the woods nearby where many elves lived, and in their hunt for small insects they came across many of the little folk and talked to them. And one day the tits that nested in the rose rambler box found an elf of great use to them.

She lived in a hole at the foot of an old oak tree. The two tits often went to hunt for insects in the bark and the elf liked their merry voices, and always popped her little golden head out to wish them good day.

One morning the tits were hunting in the oak tree bark when a gun went off not far away. It was the farmer shooting rabbits. It frightened the tits so much that they rose straight up into the air to fly – and one of them flew full-tilt into the branch overhead and hurt himself so badly that he fell down to the ground in a faint, his eyes closed, and his wings drooping.

"What's the matter, what's the matter?" called his little wife, in a fright. She flew down to her mate, but he did not move. Then she heard a scampering of feet not far off and saw

the bright-eyed weasel, whom all small creatures and birds fear, for he feasts on them.

"Help! Help!" cried the little tit, in a panic, and she flew up into the air. The weasel stopped – and then came running over to the oak tree.

But before he could snap up the poor little tit someone came rushing out of the roots of the oak. It was the golden-headed elf. She caught up the tiny tit and ran back with him into her home. He was safe there, for the weasel could not possibly squeeze into the small hole where she lived.

"I'll pay you out for that!" he shouted at her and ran off, mad with rage, for he was hungry.

In a few minutes the tit opened his
eyes and stretched his wings, none the
worse for his bump. When he found the
elf bending over him, and heard what
had happened, he was very grateful
indeed.

"It is most kind of you!" he said, in
his shrill little voice. "Most kind
indeed! Let me know, elf, if you want
help yourself at any time, and my wife
and I will be very pleased to do
whatever we can for you!"

Then he flew with his wife, back to
his nest in the box, where he rested all
day and was soon quite himself again.
When their eggs hatched out into five

pretty little youngsters, the two tits were mad with delight. They sang about them until everyone in the garden was quite tired of hearing how beautiful and how marvellous the baby tits were. But indeed they really were very sweet, for they were just bundles of blue and yellow fluff.

One day the robin brought a message to the two tits.

"Blue-tits!" he sang, "I bring a message to you from the elf in the woods. She is very unhappy and asks you to go to her."

Off went the tits at once. The elf was not in her usual place under the oak tree – but they found her shivering in the ditch not far away, with only a cobweb shawl wrapped round her.

"What is wrong?" cried the tits, flying down beside her.

"Oh, little friends," said the elf, "a dreadful thing has happened to me. The weasel was so angry because I saved the life of one of you the other day that he said he would force me to

go away. He sent an army of red ants into my cosy home and they ate up all my pretty clothes, and bit me so hard that I could not stay there any more. Now they are building their nest in the oak tree roots, so I have no home. I don't know where to go, because if I choose another hole the ants will come after me there too. Now, here I am, cold and hungry in this ditch, with only this cobweb shawl to keep me warm. I am so dreadfully afraid that the weasel will come after me."

"You poor little thing!" cried the tits, cuddling close to her. "What can we do for you? Let us think hard!"

So they thought very hard, and then the little hen tit cried out in delight.

"I know! I know! Let the elf come to live with us in our nesting-box! It is true that we are rather crowded now that we have five babies – but it is warm and cosy, and the elf will have plenty of company and be quite safe from the weasel there!"

"Oh, that would be wonderful!" said the elf, tears of joy coming into her eyes. "Oh, there is nothing in the world that I would like better! I could look after the babies for you when you went out together, couldn't I!"

"Yes, you could!" cried both tits, delighted. "There is one of our children who is far too bold. We are afraid he will climb out of the little entrance hole one day and fall to the ground. Then the weasel will be sure to get him. If *you* were living in the nest with us we should never be afraid of leaving the babies alone. Do come!"

The elf spread her pretty gleaming wings, and flew up into the air with the tits. The weasel, who was hiding in the bushes not far off, gave a snicker of rage. He had been hoping to pounce on the elf that very day.

The tits took the elf to their nesting-box. She was just too big to squeeze in through the little hole, so she had to lift up the roof and get in that way. She cuddled down among the fluffy babies and was soon as warm as toast.

How happy she was there! And how pleased all the seven tits were to have her! She was so good to them all. She looked after the five babies carefully when the two parents were away, and wouldn't let the bold one try to climb out of the hole. She saw that each baby had his share of the food in turn, and would not let the strong ones rob the weak ones. She brushed their feathers and told them tales. They loved her very much indeed.

She was very warm and cosy there, and had plenty to eat, for the little tits brought her all kinds of food each day. They knew which flowers had the sweetest honey, and they were very clever at bringing leaves with dewdrops on them, so that the elf could drink. Nobody knew that the elf lived in the box, not even the other tits. It was a secret.

And then somebody found out. Guess who it was! Yes, it was Barry. He did so badly want to see how many baby birds the tits had in the rose rambler box. So

one sunny morning he tiptoed to it, after he had seen the tit parents fly out, and he lifted up the roof-lid to see inside.

He looked down – and there, looking up at him, were five fluffy blue and yellow baby tits – and one pretty, golden-headed elf! She was cuddled down among the tits, her arms round them, the prettiest sight you could imagine!

Barry was so surprised that he simply stood and stared. Then he quietly closed the lid and went away. It

was the greatest and loveliest surprise of his life – a real secret that he couldn't tell to anyone at all.

When the parent birds came back, the elf told them what had happened. She was frightened. "I must fly off!" she said. "That boy will come back and take me away."

"No, no," sang the tits at once. "Don't be afraid of Barry. He is the nicest boy in the world! He would not harm us, and he will not harm you. You are quite safe here. Let him peep at you if he wants to. He will never, never hurt you!"

When the five baby tits flew away into the garden in the bright summer-time, the elf stayed in the nesting-box and made it her home. She tidied it up, and she made a small cupboard for herself and a shelf where she put all her belongings.

"Do come back and nest here next year," she begged the tits, who often came and peeped in at the hole to talk to her.

"We will!" they promised. "We certainly will!"

So there the elf still lives, as Barry knows very well! He peeps at her once a week, and she knows him well now and smiles gaily at him. He has never told anyone his great secret – but I know because the tits told the robin and he sang it all to me! And how I'd love to go and peep in that box – wouldn't you?

The Magic
Snow-Bird

It was holiday time, when mothers
were giving lots of parties. Jim and
Mollie had been asked to a great many,
and they were very much looking
forward to them. They had been to one,
and then a dreadful thing happened!
Baby caught chicken-pox – and that
meant no more parties for Mollie and
Jim in case they caught it too.

Wasn't it unlucky! They were so
disappointed. Mollie cried, and Jim
nearly did, but not quite. There was to
be a Christmas tree at the next two
parties they had been asked to, and
now they would miss all the fun. It was
too bad.

"Well, it's no use making a fuss," said
Mother. "You can't go and you must be
brave about it. We are all very sorry for

371

you. Look, I believe it's going to snow! You will be able to play at snowballing soon."

Sure enough, the snow was falling thickly. Mollie and Jim went to the window and watched it. It came down like big goose feathers, soft and silent. Soon the garden was covered in a white sheet.

The next morning there was a thick covering of snow everywhere, and the two children shouted with delight.

"We'll build a snowman! We'll snow-ball the paper-boy! We'll build a little snow-hut!"

"Put on your wellington boots, your thick coats, and woolly caps," said Mother. "Then you can go and do what you like."

So out they went. How lovely it was! Their feet made big marks in the snow, and when they kicked it, it flew up into the air like powder.

"Let's build a snowman first," said Jim. So they began. They made big balls of snow by rolling them down the

lawn. They got bigger and bigger, and then, when they were nice and large, Jim used two for the snowman's body and one for his head.

They put a hat on his head, and a pipe in his mouth, stones down his front for buttons, and old gloves on his snowy hands. He did look funny. Mother laughed when she saw him.

"Now what shall we make," asked Jim. "What about a snow-bird, Mollie? Do you remember how we made a bird at school out of clay? It was quite easy. Let's make a big one out of snow!"

"Yes, nobody makes snow-birds!" said Mollie. "How surprised everyone will be!"

So they began. First they made a round body. Then they put the bird's long neck on. After that they made a head with a beak of wood sticking out. Then they gave him a long tail sweeping down to the ground. He stood on two wooden legs, and had two stones for eyes, so he looked very grand indeed.

"Isn't he wonderful!" cried Mollie.

"Just look at him, Jim! Let's call Daddy and Mummy, they'll be so surprised."

They went to call them, and soon their parents came out into the garden to see the bird. They thought he was magnificent.

Now, just at that very moment a bright blue kingfisher flashed by. He had come from the river, and was going to a nice pool he knew, which he hoped would not be quite frozen over. As he passed over the snow-bird, he dropped one of his blue feathers. It floated down, and stuck in the snow-bird's head, just on the top, so that he looked as if he had a funny little crest.

"Oh, look!" cried Mollie. "He's got a blue feather on his top-knot! Doesn't he look funny!"

"Leave it there," said Mother. "King-fishers' feathers are lucky."

So they left it, and went in to lunch. It was still there when they went out to play afterwards. This time they made a nice little hut with a door and window. It was just big enough for the two of

them. Jim and Mollie were sorry when the sun went and the garden began to get dark.

"We shall have to go in to tea soon," said Jim, looking out of the little snow-window. Then he suddenly said "Oh!" and sat very still, staring hard.

"What's the matter?" said Mollie.

"Shh!" said Jim, in a whisper. "Keep still. I saw something strange."

"Oh, *what*?" asked Mollie. "Quick, tell me."

"I thought I saw the snow-bird stretch its wings," said Jim, in astonishment. "But look – he's quite still now, isn't he, Mollie?"

"Yes, quite," said Mollie. "Oh, Jim! Did you really see that?"

"Well, I *thought* I did," said Jim. "Let's watch and see if he moves again." They watched quietly for a few minutes and then they were called in to tea, and in they had to go. They told Mother what they thought had happened, and she laughed.

"Well, maybe that kingfisher's

377

feather has put some magic into the snow-bird," she said. "Everybody knows that there's something strange about kingfishers' feathers."

"That must be it!" thought the two children. "What a funny thing!"

After tea they went to the kitchen window, and tried to see out into the garden. It was dark, but they could just make out the snowman, the snow-hut and the snow-bird. As they peered out into the darkness, they heard a peculiar noise.

"It sounds like some sort of bird," said Mollie. "Could it be the snow-bird whistling, Jim? It's a kind of singing-whistling noise all mixed up."

"Let's go and see," said Jim. So they scrambled down from the window, and ran to put on their coats. Then they slipped out into the garden.

"Yes, it is the snow-bird!" said Jim, in astonishment. "It must be magic, Mollie."

They went close up to him. He gleamed white in the darkness, and his two stony eyes shone brightly.

"Look!" said Jim, "he's opening and shutting his wings! He's come alive!"

The snow-bird stared at them solemnly. He stood first on one leg, and then on the other. Then he flapped his

white wings, and stood on tiptoe.

"Hello, hello, hello!" he said. "It's nice of you to come and see me. I was just feeling rather lonely."

"Are you magic?" asked Mollie, who was just a bit frightened.

"I am rather," answered the bird. "It's all because of that kingfisher's feather, you know. It's very lucky, and it's very magic. It would make anything come alive!"

"Are you going to fly away?" asked Jim. "Where will you go to, if you do?"

"All snow-birds, snowmen, and snow-animals belong to the country of the North Wind," said the bird. "It's a fine land too. It's where Santa Claus lives, you know. The toys are made there by goblins and dwarfs, the Christmas trees grow there, already decorated with toys—"

"What! Do they grow with toys on them?" cried the children. "We've only seen the kind that you buy, and dress up with toys yourself."

"Pooh," said the bird. "Those are

stupid. You should just see the ones that grow out in the country of the North Wind! I shall see some tonight, if I go."

"We were going to some parties where there would be lovely Christmas trees covered with toys," said Jim. "But now Baby's got chicken-pox, and we can't. I do wish we could go with you, and see some trees growing with toys already on them."

"Well, why not?" said the bird, spreading its white wings. "There's plenty of room on my back, isn't there? You can both sit there comfortably, while I fly. I'll bring you back safely enough."

"Oh!" cried both children in delight. "What an adventure!"

"You may find me rather cold to sit on," said the bird. "I'm made of snow, you know. You'd better get a cushion to put on my back, then you won't feel cold."

Jim ran to the house and fetched a big cushion from his bedroom. He popped it on the snow-bird's back, and then he and Mollie climbed on. The bird spread its wings, and then *whoosh!* he rose into the air!

Mollie and Jim held on tight. Their hearts were beating very fast, but they were enjoying themselves enormously.

The bird went at a fearful rate, and the children had to pull their woolly caps well down over their ears. They looked downwards, but the earth was too dark for them to see anything except little spots of light here and there.

After a long time, the bird turned its head round to them.

"Nearly there!" he said. "Isn't this fun!"

"Yes!" shouted the children. "Oh look! Everything is getting lighter. The sun is rising!"

"Yes, we've gone so fast and far that we've met him again!" said the bird. "I'm going to land now, so hold tight. You'll be able to see everything quite well soon."

Down he went, and down. Then *bump*! he landed on the snowy ground. Jim and Mollie jumped off his back. There was sunlight everywhere and they could see everything clearly.

"We haven't much time," said the snow-bird. "This is where the goblins live who make the rocking-horses for you."

He took the children to some big caves in a nearby hill, and Jim and Mollie saw hundreds of tiny goblins busily hammering, painting and putting rockers and manes on fine rocking-horses. The funny thing was that the

horses seemed alive, and neighed and kicked and stamped all the time.

The children watched in astonishment. Then the snow-bird asked if they might have a ride on one of the horses, and the goblins said yes, certainly. So up they jumped, and off went the horse with them, rocking all over the cave. Jim and Mollie loved it.

Then the bird took them to where the doll's-houses were being built by tiny pixies. The pixies lived in them, and Mollie thought it was lovely to see them sitting at the little tables on tiny chairs, peeping out of the windows, and sleeping in the small beds.

"Now hurry up, or we shan't have time to see the Christmas trees growing," said the snow-bird. "Jump on my back again. They're not far away."

He took them to a huge field spread with snow. In it were rows and rows of Christmas trees, some very tiny, some bigger, and some so big that Jim and Mollie had to bend their heads back to see the tops.

"Look at the tiny ones," said Jim. "They have got little buds on them. Are the buds going to grow into toys, snow-bird?"

"Yes, they are," said the snow-bird. "Look at the next row. They are bigger still."

The children looked. They went from row to row, and saw the toys getting bigger and bigger as the trees grew in size. At first they were tight little buds. Then they loosened a little, and Jim and Mollie could make out a tiny doll or a little engine. The next size trees had toys a little bigger, and the largest trees of all were dressed with the biggest, loveliest things you could imagine! Fairy dolls, big books, fine engines, great boxes of soldiers, footballs and all kind of things hung there!

"Will the little trees grow into big trees like this, with all the toys the right size?" asked Mollie.

"Of course," said the snow-bird. "Then people buy them. Look, this tree

387

is bought by someone. It has a label on it. It is to be fetched tomorrow."

Jim read the label.

FOR JACK BROWN'S PARTY, it said.

"Oh!" cried Mollie. "Why, that's the party we were going to tomorrow! To think that this lovely tree is going to be there! Oh, I wish we were going!"

Her eyes filled with tears, and the snow-bird was terribly upset.

"Don't, please don't," he begged. "Look, you shall have a little Christ-

mas tree seed for your own. Plant it, and it will grow into a good size by next Christmas!"

"And have toys on, too?" asked Mollie.

"Certainly," said the bird. He pressed something into Mollie's hand. She took it. It was a tiny silver ball, the sort you see on Christmas cakes.

"Thank you," said Mollie. "I'll be sure to plant it carefully. What fun to have a Christmas tree of my own, with toys and everything on!"

"Now it's time we went back," said the snow-bird. "It's nearly seven o'clock by your time, and your mother will want to put you to bed. Jump up again, my dears."

Up they climbed, and once more the snow-bird flew back into the darkness, leaving the sun far behind him. The wind blew hard, and the children held on tightly, afraid of being blown off.

"Pff! Isn't the wind strong!" cried the bird. Then suddenly he gave a terrible cry.

"Oh, whatever is it?" cried Mollie.

"The wind has blown away the kingfisher's feather on my head!" cried the bird. "The magic's going out of me! I shall soon be nothing but a bird made of snow. Oh, oh, I hope you get home safely before that happens!"

390

He flew more and more slowly, and it seemed to the frightened children as if he were becoming colder and colder. At last he gave a pant, and fell to earth. The children tumbled off, and rolled on the snowy ground. Then they picked themselves up, and looked round.

"Are we home, or not?" asked Jim. "I can't see the snow-hut or the snow-man, can you, Mollie?"

"No," said Mollie. "But look, Jim! Isn't that our summerhouse? Yes, it is! I can just see the weathercock on the top by the light of the stars. We're at the bottom of the garden. The poor old snow-bird couldn't quite get back to the lawn he started from!"

"He's changed into snow and nothing else," said Jim. "What a pity that blue feather got blown away."

"Children, children, didn't you hear me call?" cried Mother crossly, from the window. "What are you doing out there in the dark? You know you ought to be inside by the fire! Come in at once!"

Jim and Mollie picked up the cushion

391

and ran indoors. They tried to explain to Mother where they had been, and all about the magic snow-bird, but she was too cross to listen. She just popped them into bed, and left them.

But do you know, in the morning the snow-bird was standing at the bottom of the garden, and not in the place where Father and Mother had seen him the day before.

"There you are!" cried Jim. "That just proves we are telling the truth, Mummy. How could he have got down there by himself? That shows he did take us last night, and couldn't quite get back to the right place."

"Don't be silly," said Mother. "You moved him yourself when you went out to play in the dark after tea yesterday."

"Well, anyhow, I've still got that Christmas tree seed that the snow-bird gave me," said Mollie. "I shall plant it, Mummy, and then you'll soon see we are speaking the truth, for it will grow into a proper Christmas tree, all decorated with lovely toys."

She ran out and planted it in her
own little garden. Nothing has come up
yet, because it was only a week ago –
but wouldn't you love to see everyone's
surprise when it really grows into a
beautiful Christmas tree, with a fairy
doll at the top, and engines, books,
teddy bears and other toys hanging all
over it?

The Cat
Without Whiskers

Inky was a black cat, with the finest white whiskers in the street. He was a handsome cat, with sharp ears and a long thick tail that looked like a snake when he waved it to and fro. He had a white mark under his chin which the children called his bib, and he washed it three times a day, so that it was always like snow.

Inky was plump, for he was the best ratter and mouser in the town, and never lacked a good dinner. When he sat on the wall washing himself he was a fine sight, for his glossy fur gleamed in the sun and his whiskers stuck out each side of his face like white wires.

"I'm the finest-looking cat in the town," said Inky proudly, and he looked scornfully down at the tabby in the garden below, and the white cat washing itself on a windowsill near by. "Nobody is as good-looking as me!"

Then a little boy came by, and when he saw the big black cat sitting up on the wall, he shouted up at him, laughing, "Hello, Whiskers!"

Inky was offended. His name wasn't Whiskers. It was Inky. A little girl heard what the boy said and she laughed. "That's a good name for him," she said.

"He's a very whiskery cat. Whiskers!"

Everyone thought it a funny name, and soon Inky was being called Whiskers all day long, even by the cats and dogs around. This made him really very angry.

"It's a horrible, silly name," he thought crossly, "and it's rude of people to call me that. They don't call that nice old gentleman with the beard 'Whiskers', do they? And they don't shout 'Nosy' at that boy with the big nose. I shan't answer them when they call me Whiskers!"

So he didn't – but it wasn't any good, for everyone shouted "Whiskers! Whiskers!" as soon as they saw Inky's wonderful whiskers.

Inky thought hard. "I shall get rid of my whiskers," he said to himself. "Yes – I shall start a new fashion for cats. We won't have whiskers. After all, men shave every morning, and people think that is a good idea. I will shave my whiskers off, and then no one will call me Whiskers."

He told his idea to wise old Shellyback the tortoise. Shellyback listened and pulled at the grass he was eating.

"It is best not to meddle with things you have been given," he said. "You will be sorry."

"No, I shan't," said Inky. "My whiskers are no use to me that I can see – I shall shave them off!"

Well, he slipped into the bathroom at his home early the next morning and found the thing his master called a razor. In an instant Inky had shaved off his beautiful whiskers. They were gone. He

was no longer a whiskery cat.

He looked at himself in the glass. He did look a bit strange – but at any rate no one would now shout "Whiskers" after him. He slipped down the stairs and out into the garden. He jumped on the wall in the sun.

The milkman came by and looked at him. He did not shout "Whiskers!" as he usually did. He stared in rather a puzzled way and said nothing at all. Then a young boy came by delivering papers, and he didn't shout "Whiskers!" either.

Inky was pleased. At last he had got rid of his horrible name. He sat in the sun, purring, and soon his friends gathered round him. There was Tabby from next door, the white cat Snowball, Shellyback the tortoise, who looked up at him from the lawn, and the old dog Rover, who never chased cats.

"What's the matter with you this morning, Inky?" asked Snowball, puzzled. "You look different."

"His whiskers are gone," said Tabby, startled. "How strange."

"How did you lose them?" asked Rover.

"I shaved them off," Inky said proudly. "I am starting a new fashion for cats. Grown-up men shave their whiskers off each day, don't they? Well, why should cats have whiskers? Don't you think I look much smarter now?"

Everyone stared at Inky, but nobody said a word. They all thought Inky looked dreadful without his whiskers.

"You'll soon see everyone following my fashion of no whiskers," said Inky. "It's much more comfortable. Whiskers always get in my way when I'm washing my face, but now I can wash it as smoothly as anything. Look!" He washed his face with his paw. Certainly it looked easier to do it without whiskers. But the older animals shook their heads.

"Whiskers must be some use or we wouldn't have them," said Tabby.

"Well, what use are they?" said Inky.

But nobody was clever enough to think of anything to say in answer to that. One by one they slipped off to their homes to dinner, quite determined that they were not going to shave off their whiskers, whatever Inky did.

Now that night Inky felt very hungry. He had been late for tea that afternoon and a stray dog had gone into his garden and eaten up the plate of fish and milk that his mistress had put out for him. Inky was annoyed.

"Never mind," he thought to himself. "I'll go hunting tonight. I'll catch a few mice and perhaps a rat or two. I know a good place in the hedge at the bottom of the garden. I'll hide on one side of it and wait for the night animals to come out."

So off he went when darkness came and crouched down on one side of the hedge. Soon he heard the pitter-pattering of little mice-feet. Inky stiffened and kept quite still. In a moment he would squeeze through the hedge and pounce on those foolish mice.

He took a step forward. His paw was like velvet and made no noise. He pushed his head into a hole in the hedge – then his body – but alas for Inky! His body was too big for the hole, and the hedge

creaked as he tried to get through. The mice heard the noise and shot off into their holes. Not one was left.

"Bother!" said Inky crossly. "I'll wait again. I believe that old rat has a run here somewhere. I'd like to catch him!"

So he waited – and sure enough the big rat ran silently by the hedge. Inky heard him and began to creep towards him; but his fat body brushed against some leaves and the rat heard and fled.

Inky was astonished. Usually he could hunt marvellously without making a single sound. Why was it that his body seemed so clumsy tonight? Why did he brush against things and make rustling noises? It was most annoying.

And then suddenly he knew the reason why. Although he hadn't thought about it, his fine whiskers had always helped him to hunt. They had stretched out each side of his face, and were just about the width of his body. He had known that if he could get his head and whiskers through a hole without touching anything, his body would go through easily too, without a sound.

"It was my whiskers that helped my body to know if it could go easily and silently through the holes and between leaves," thought Inky in despair. "Of course! Why didn't I think of that before? They were just the right width for my body, and I knew quite well if I touched anything with my whiskers that my body would also touch it and make a noise – and so I would go another way!"

Inky was quite right. His whiskers had helped him in his hunting. Now he would not be able to hunt well, for he would never know if his body could squeeze through gaps and holes. He would always be making rustling, crackling noises with

403

leaves and twigs. He would never catch anything. Poor Inky!

You can guess that Inky was always waiting for his mistress to put out his dinner after that – for he hardly ever caught a mouse or rat now. He grew much thinner, and he hid himself away, for he was ashamed to think that he had shaved off the things that had been so useful to him.

"A new fashion indeed!" thought Inky. "I was mad! If only I had my lovely whiskers again I wouldn't mind being called "Whiskers" a hundred times a day. My life is spoilt. I shall never be able to hunt again."

He was a sad and unhappy cat, ashamed to talk to anyone except wise old Shellyback the tortoise. One day he told Shellyback why he was unhappy. Shellyback looked at him closely and laughed.

"Go and sit up on the wall in the sun and see what happens," he said to Inky. "You'll find your troubles are not so big as you thought they were."

404

In surprise Inky jumped up on the wall
and sat there in the sun. The milkman
came by with his cart. He looked up.

"Hello, Whiskers!" he shouted.
"Good old Whiskers!"

Inky nearly fell off the wall in
astonishment. What! He was called
Whiskers again even if he had shaved

them off? But silly old Inky had quite forgotten something. What had he forgotten?

He had forgotten that whiskers grow again like hair. His whiskers had grown out fine and long and strong and white – and he had been so miserable that he hadn't even noticed. Silly old Whiskers!

He was happy when he found that he had them again. He sat and purred so loudly that Shellyback really thought there was an aeroplane flying somewhere near! It sounded just like it.

And now Inky can hunt again, and is the best mouser in the town. He has grown plump and handsome, and his whiskers are finer than ever. He loves to hear himself called Whiskers now. So if you see him up on the wall, black and shining, don't say "Hello, Inky!" – shout "Good old Whiskers!" and he'll purr like a kettle on the boil!

Tarrydiddle Town

Sarah lived with her mother and father right on the edge of a magic wood. Her mother often warned her not to go wandering too far into the wood, in case she disturbed the fairy folk, and made them cross.

"I *should* like to follow that little twisty path under the oak trees," said Sarah to her mother one day.

"Hush, child! Never think of such a thing!" said her mother sharply. "And you must keep indoors with me today and help me make the bread."

Sarah pouted and sulked. She was a dreadfully lazy little girl, and she didn't want to stay indoors at all. So when her mother was not looking she slipped out and ran into the wood.

"I *will* follow that little twisty path!"

she said to herself, and she ran down the little path under the big oak trees. It became darker and darker, for the wood grew thick and kept out the sunshine.

Suddenly Sarah heard voices, and crept behind a tree, a little afraid.

"The king says we *must* be cleaner and tidier," said a voice crossly. "I can't think how we're going to manage it!"

"If only we could find a servant," sighed another voice; "but nobody ever comes to Tarrydiddle Town." Just then a twig that Sarah was treading on suddenly snapped with a loud noise.

"Someone's there!" cried the voices, and Sarah heard rushing feet.

Then two strange-looking creatures appeared in front of her, and seized hold of her wrists. They had big heads with very thick hair, long noses, and wide mouths. Their bodies were small and their feet large.

"Who are you," cried one creature, "and what are you doing in our part of the wood?"

408

"I'm Sarah," said Sarah; "and do let me go, you're hurting."

"Can you sweep?" suddenly asked the other creature.

"Yes," answered Sarah.

"And clean windows, and make beds?"

"Oh yes, yes!" said Sarah crossly; "but why are you asking me such silly questions?"

"Splendid!" cried the two creatures. "We'll have you for a servant! Come along with us!" and they dragged Sarah off.

"Where are you taking me?" asked Sarah.

"To Tarrydiddle Town," they answered. "The King of Fairyland visited us the other day, and said our town was so dreadfully untidy and dirty that if we didn't make it better he would punish us. But it's been untidy for so long that we've forgotten how to make it bright and clean."

"Well, I'd like to visit Tarrydiddle Town," said Sarah, "but I'm not going to be your servant, so there!"

"We have cream cakes and treacle pudding at every meal," said one Tarrydiddle.

"Oh!" said Sarah, "I'd love to go to your town. Let's hurry up and go!"

When the Tarrydiddles saw that Sarah was eager to go with them they were very pleased. They hurried along until they came to a little stream, on which rocked a canoe.

"Jump in!" cried the two peculiar

creatures to Sarah. She jumped in, and off went the boat down the stream with the three of them.

The stream soon left the wood, and came out into open fields. Presently,

away in the distance, Sarah saw the oddest village that ever was built.

The houses, all of them small, were higgledypiggledy and crooked. The chimneys were not only on the roofs, but sometimes stuck out of the walls. Some of the houses had doors very

411

high up, but with no steps up to them. Sarah wondered however the people got into them.

"Here we are!" said the Tarrydiddles, jumping out. Sarah jumped out too.

"Well!" she said, as she came near the town. "Well, I never saw such a strange, untidy, dirty place in my life! Just *look* at the windows! They're thick with dirt! And the windowsills! Absolutely black!"

Sarah wandered round Tarrydiddle town for a good while. The streets were crooked and wanted sweeping, for there were all sorts of papers flying about.

"I'll peep into a few houses now," said Sarah. She walked into one, and found the floor dirty with mud. There was dust on everything, and all the curtains wanted washing.

"Ugh!" said Sarah, walking out. "What a horrid place Tarrydiddle Town is! I shan't stay *here* long!"

Soon she came to a street of shops, and to her delight there were rows and

rows of cream cakes and big plates of steaming hot treacle pudding.

"You can go and have anything in the shop you like!" one of the Tarrydiddles told her. "We don't pay for anything here."

Sarah ran in, and ate five cream cakes and two plates of treacle pudding! At the end she said, "Now I want to go home, please."

"Oh no, you can't," said the Tarrydiddles. "You must stop and work for us, and show us how to make our town clean."

Sarah stamped and roared and frowned and sulked, but it was all no use. The lazy little girl had to do what she was told. She was taken to the biggest house in the town and told to put it straight. How she wished she had stayed at home and helped her mother!

"Well, I'll try to clean the house," said Sarah tearfully; "but will you let me go home afterwards?"

"You must stay here a week," said the Tarrydiddles, "for the king is coming then. If he says our town is tidy and clean we'll let you go home. If not, you must stay till the king comes again, and that may not be for months and months."

"Only a week!" exclaimed Sarah. "Why, I can't possibly get things clean and tidy in a week! You are *horrid*, you Tarrydiddles!"

Sarah began working as quickly as she could. She *was* so afraid the king would come and say Tarrydiddle Town was untidy, and then she wouldn't be able to go home.

"I'll scrub all the floors," said Sarah to herself. So she got a pail of water, and scrubbed the floors of the little house till they shone.

"How clever! How beautiful!" said all the Tarrydiddles, watching. And they ran straight home and scrubbed all *their* floors to see if they could make them shine too. Then Sarah dusted all the walls and all the furniture, and polished it till she could see herself in the table and chair legs.

"How wonderful!" exclaimed the Tarrydiddles, and off they all went to do the same.

The next day Sarah pulled down all the curtains and tablecloths, and washed them all as white as snow in a big wash-tub of hot water. They looked simply lovely all hanging out on the line to dry.

All Tarrydiddle Town was busy washing too, and copying Sarah.

"How clever you are! How clever!" they kept saying to Sarah, who was beginning to feel rather pleased with the way the house looked.

All through the week Sarah could find nothing to eat but cream cakes and treacle pudding. At last she grew so tired of them that she could hardly bear to look at them.

"Oh, if only I could taste some of mother's home-made bread!" she sighed. "Oh, I *do* hope the king will think things are tidy, and I can go home!"

She cleaned the windows, and

416

whitened the windowsills, and blacked the grates.

"Beautiful! Wonderful!" said all the funny little Tarrydiddles, going off to do the same in their own houses.

Then came the last day. Sarah looked all over the house, and could find nothing dirty, and nothing untidy. Everything shone and glittered.

Tomorrow the king is coming, she thought. I must bake some bread, and get the streets cleaned today, and then that's really all!

She caught up a broom, and hurried outside.

"Clever girl! Marvellous girl!" cried the Tarrydiddles, watching her. "Why didn't *we* think of sweeping the streets?" And soon all of them were sweeping too, and the streets were as clean as clean.

Sarah made some bread after that, as she thought the king might like something else to eat besides the everlasting cream cakes and treacle pudding. After that she was so tired that

417

she dropped asleep in the kitchen.

"Oh, how lovely everything looks!" she cried next morning as she went round the town, and saw all the houses clean and tidy and neat, like the one she herself had lived in. "There's only one thing left to do!"

"What's that?" cried the Tarrydiddles, crowding round her.

"Wash yourselves, and brush your
hair," said Sarah. They all went off to
do it.

Tara! Tan-tan-tara! Tara!

"The king! The king!" shouted all the
Tarrydiddles, rushing out clean and
tidy to meet the king and his courtiers.
Sarah went too.

"Greetings to you, people of Tarrydiddle Town," said the grand King of
Fairyland. And then His Majesty went
into every house to see if it were tidy
and clean.

"Splendid! Marvellous!" cried the
king, as he went into one after
another. "Who has helped you to do all
this?"

"Sarah has! Sarah has!" shouted the
Tarrydiddles, dragging her forward.

"You have done splendid work," said
the king. "I will grant you a wish.
What would you like?"

"Oh, may I go home again, please?"
begged Sarah. "I'm so tired of cream

419

cakes and treacle pudding, and I can only bake bread myself. I'll never be lazy again."

"Yes, you may go home," said the king kindly; "and if Tarrydiddle Town ever gets dirty again, I shall know whom to send for to put it right, shan't

I, Tarrydiddles? So be careful to keep your houses spick and span in future!"

He waved his wand. A great wind rushed round Sarah and carried her away. Then *bump*! she was standing on the ground again in front of her mother's cottage.

"Mummy! Mummy!" called Sarah, rushing in. "I've come home, and I'll never be lazy again."

And if you ever meet a little girl who can't bear to eat cream cakes or treacle pudding, ask if her name is Sarah, and whether she has heard anything more of Tarrydiddle Town.

The
Bubble Airships

Once upon a time, when Jack took his bubble-blower and bowl of soapy water into the garden, he had a strange adventure. He sat down by the old oak-tree, mixed up his water, and began to blow big rainbow bubbles.

The adventure began when one of the bubbles floated upwards and disappeared inside the big hole in the middle of the old oak-tree. Jack watched it go there – and no sooner had he seen it pop inside the tree than he heard a great many excited little voices coming from the tree itself!

The little boy listened in astonishment. Who could be inside the tree? He climbed up and peeped inside – but it was too dark to see anything, and as soon as the little folk inside heard him climbing up, they became quite quiet. Not a word could he hear!

"This is a funny thing," thought Jack, in excitement. "I must get my torch and light up the hollow in the tree – then I may see something lovely!"

He ran to get his torch. He climbed up the tree once more and shone his torch into the hole – and there, at the very bottom of the old tree, deep down inside the hollow trunk, Jack saw a crowd of tiny, frightened pixies, all looking up at him with pale, scared faces!

The little boy stared in amazement.

He had never in his life seen a pixie before – and here were about twenty, all squeezed up together!

"What are you doing inside this tree?" he asked. "Do you live here?"

The pixies chattered together in high, twittering voices. "Shall we tell him, shall we tell him?" they cried. Then one of the pixies looked up at Jack and said, "Little boy, you have a kind face. We will tell you why we are here. The green goblins caught us yesterday and cut off our wings. They wanted us to tell them all the magic spells we knew, and because we wouldn't they shut us up in this hollow tree."

"But why can't you get out?" asked Jack.

"Well, our wings are gone," said the pixie sorrowfully, "so we can't fly – and the tree is much too difficult to climb inside – so here we are, prisoners – and the goblins will come again tonight to try and make us tell them what we know."

"I'm sorry about your wings," said Jack. "Won't you ever be able to fly again?"

"Oh yes," said another pixie. "They will grow again – but not for four weeks."

"What were you so excited about just now?" asked Jack. "I was blowing bubbles when I suddenly heard you chattering away in here, and that's what made me come and look."

"Well, one of your bubbles suddenly blew down into the tree," said a pixie. "And it gave us such a surprise. We grabbed at it – but it broke and made us all wet!"

"I wish I could get you out," said Jack. "But I can't possibly reach down to you – the tree is so big, and you are right down at the bottom."

"No, we shall have to stay locked up here," said the pixies sadly.

But suddenly one of the pixies gave a shout and cried, "I know! Could the little boy blow some bubbles down into the tree for us? Because if he could, we might make some buckets of grass and fix them to the bubbles – get into the baskets and float off!"

"Good idea!" shouted everyone. "Little boy, will you do it?"

"Yes, rather!" cried Jack. "I'll go and pick you some grass first. Then you can be weaving little baskets of it while I fetch my soapy water and my bubble-blower. I shall have to be careful not to spill the water when I climb up the tree!"

In a short while Jack had picked some grass and dropped it down to the pixies. They at once began to weave strong little baskets with their tiny fingers – baskets quite big and strong enough to carry

them away! Jack climbed down again and picked up his water and bubble-blower. Very carefully he climbed up the tree once more, holding his bowl of water in one hand, and pulling himself up the tree with the other.

He carried his bubble-blower in his mouth, so that was quite safe. He switched on his torch and looked down into the tree again. The pixies had made some beautiful baskets, with long blades of grass sticking up from them for ropes.

"You will be able to make lovely airships with those baskets hung beneath my bubbles," cried the little boy. He blew a big blue-and-green bubble and puffed it into the tree. A small pixie held up his green basket to it as it floated down. The grass caught on to the soapy bubble and the basket swung there, just like the underneath of an airship! The pixie

climbed into it, and the others gave him a gentle push. Off he floated up the tree, and as soon as he came out into the sunshine, Jack blew the bubble away from the leaves and branches so that it would not burst. It floated gently to the ground and burst there with a little pop!

The pixie tumbled out of the basket on to the ground, laughing in delight to think he had escaped from the tree.

Jack blew some more big bubbles, and they floated down the hole in the tree. Some of them burst before they reached the pixies, for they bumped against the sides of the tree, but those that reached the bottom had the grass buckets fixed to them in a trice – and then up came the pixies, each in his own little bubble airship!

Jack laughed to see them. They really did look funny, floating along in their tiny airships. The last pixie of all had no one to push him out of the hollow tree and he broke two or three bubbles trying to push himself off; but at last he managed to float upwards too, and soon he was on

the grass with the others, laughing and
talking in excitement.

"We shall run away to a rabbit-hole
we know and hide there till our wings
have grown," said a pixie to Jack. "It's
so kind of you to have helped us.
Goodbye! We may see you again some
day! Won't those goblins be angry
tonight when they find we have gone!"

They all ran off and left Jack alone with his bubble-blower. How excited he was to think of his strange adventure with it! Who would have thought that he could blow bubble airships?

The pixies rewarded Jack for his kindness. They found out where his little garden was, and they kept it well-weeded and well-watered for him, and made his flowers the biggest and loveliest in the garden. I know, because I have seen them!

The Big Juicy
Carrot

One fine morning, Bobtail, the rabbit,
met Long-ears, the hare, and they set
off together, talking about this and
that.

They stopped by a hedge and lay
quiet, for they could hear a cart
passing. Bobtail peeped through and
saw that it was a farm-cart, laden with
carrots and turnips. How his mouth
watered!

And then, just as the cart passed
where the two animals were crouching,
a wheel ran over a great stone, and the
jerk made a big, juicy, orange carrot fall
from the cart to the ground. The hare
and the rabbit looked at it in great
delight.

When the cart had gone out of sight
the two of them hurried into the lane.

Bobtail picked up the carrot. Long-ears spoke eagerly:

"We both saw it at once. We must share it!"

"Certainly!" said Bobtail. "I will break it in half!"

So he broke the carrot in half – but although each piece measured the same, one bit was the thick top part of the carrot, and the other was the thin bottom part. Bobtail picked up the top part – but Long-ears stopped him.

"One piece is bigger than the other," he said. "There is no reason why *you* should have the bigger piece, cousin."

"And no reason why *you* should, either!" the rabbit said crossly.

"Give it to me!" squealed the hare.

"Certainly *not*!" said the rabbit. They each glared at the other, but neither dared to do any more.

"We had better ask someone to judge between us," said the hare, at last. "Whom shall we ask?"

Bobtail looked all round, but he could see no one but Neddy the donkey, peering over the hedge at them.

"There isn't anyone in sight except stupid old Neddy," he said. "It's not much good asking *him*. He has no brains to speak of!"

"That's true," said Long-ears. "He's an old stupid, everyone knows that. But who else is there to ask?"

"No one," said Bobtail. "Well come on. Let's take the carrot to the donkey and ask him to choose which of us shall have the larger piece."

434

So they ran through the hole in the hedge and went up to Neddy. He had heard every word they said and was not at all pleased to be thought so stupid.

The two creatures told him what they wanted.

"If I am so stupid as you think, I wonder you want me to judge," said Neddy, blinking at them.

"Well, you will have to do," said the rabbit. "Now tell us – how are we to know which of us shall have the bigger piece?"

"I can soon put that right for you, even with *my* poor brain!" said Neddy. He took the larger piece in his mouth and bit off the end.

"Perhaps that will have made them the same size!" he said, crunching up the juicy bit of carrot he had bitten off.

But no – he had bitten off such a big piece that now the piece that *had* been the larger one was smaller than the other!

"Soon put *that* right!" said Neddy,

and he picked up the second piece. He bit a large piece off that one, and then dropped it. But now it was much smaller than the first piece!

The hare and the rabbit watched in alarm. This was dreadful!

"Stop, Neddy!" said Long-ears. "Give us what is left. You have no right to crunch up our carrot!"

"Well, I am only trying to help you!"

said Neddy indignantly. "Wait a moment. Perhaps *this* time I'll make the pieces equal."

He took another bite at a piece of carrot – oh dear, such a big bite this time! The two animals were in despair.

"Give us the rest!" they begged. "Do not eat any more!"

"Well," said Neddy, looking at the last two juicy pieces, and keeping his foot on them so that the two animals could not get them. "What about my payment for troubling to settle your quarrel? What will you give me for that?"

"Nothing at all!" cried Long-ears.

"What! Nothing at all?" said Neddy, in anger. "Very well, then – I shall take my own payment!"

And with that he put his head down and took up the rest of the carrot! Chomp-chomp-chomp! He crunched it all up with great enjoyment.

"Thanks!" he said to Long-ears and Bobtail. "That was very nice. I'm obliged to you."

He cantered away to the other side of the field, and as he went, he brayed loudly with laughter. The two big-eyed creatures looked at one another.

"Bobtail," said Long-ears, "do you think that donkey was as stupid as we thought he was?"

"No, I don't," groaned Bobtail. "He was much cleverer than we were – and you know, Long-ears, if one of us had been sensible, we would *both* now be nibbling carrot – instead of seeing that stupid donkey chewing it all up!"

They ran off – Bobtail to his hole and Long-ears to the field where he had his home. As for Neddy, he put his head over the wall and told his friend, the brown horse, all about that big juicy carrot.

You *should* have heard them laugh!

A Tale of Two Boys
and a Kitten

Geoffrey was in bed with a bad cold. He coughed and he sneezed, and he felt very sorry for himself indeed.

"You'll soon feel better," said his mother. "You feel horrid today, but tomorrow you'll want to sit up and eat jelly and drink orange squash, and play with your soldiers."

Mother was right, of course. Next day Geoffrey did feel better. In fact, he wanted to get up.

"No," said Mother. "Not yet. Look, here is a walking-stick beside your bed. When you want anything, bang on the floor with it and I shall hear. There isn't a bell you can use."

Geoffrey didn't want to bang more often than he could help because he knew that his mother was very busy.

He tried to think of all the things he wanted, so that his mother could bring them all at the same time, and not have to bother with him after that.

"My soldiers, please," he said. "And my drawing-book, Mummy. And my pencil and rubber. And could I have Paddy-Paws, too?"

Paddy-Paws, as you can guess, was the kitten. She was about six months old, and as merry and bright as could be. She loved Geoffrey. He never teased her or pulled her tail as the next-door boy did when he came to play.

"Yes, you can have Paddy-Paws," said Mother. "She misses you very much. I'll bring her with all the other things you want."

So very soon the kitten was prancing about Geoffrey's bed, playing with his soldiers, knocking them over as soon as he stood them up!

"We're playing enemies," Geoffrey told her. "I have to stand them up to fight, and you have to knock them down!"

440

Paddy-Paws easily won that game. Then, quite suddenly, Geoffrey felt sick. He looked for the stick to knock on the floor. It had fallen down. Oh dear – if he leaned out of bed to get it he would certainly be sick! He lay down flat, hoping it would pass off.

Paddy-Paws crept up to him. She knew he was feeling horrid. He looked at her and a thought came into his head. Couldn't she fetch his mother for him?

He took his pencil and scribbled a note on a bit of drawing paper. He found a piece of string round a parcel on his bedside table, made a hole in the paper and ran the string through it. Then he tied the note round the kitten's neck.

"Go quickly and take it to Mummy," he said to Paddy-Paws. "Fetch Mummy!"

He pushed the kitten off the bed and she leaped to the floor. She turned and looked at him. What was it Geoffrey wanted her to do? What was this thing round her neck? Then she turned and padded out of the room. Down the stairs she went and into the kitchen. Mother was there baking cakes. Paddy-Paws ran up to her, mewing.

Mother looked down and saw the note tied round her neck at once. She slipped it off. *Mummy, I feel sick*, said the note. Mother got a basin and ran upstairs at top speed. Geoffrey soon felt better again. He leaned back on his pillow.

"You came just in time," he said. "I was so afraid I'd make a mess that you'd have to clear up. Mummy, did Paddy-Paws bring the note?"

"Yes, the clever little thing," said Mother. "See if she will bring a note another time, if you want anything!"

Well, Geoffrey sat up again in a little while, and picked up his drawing-book to try and draw the kitten. She sat looking at him, as pretty as a picture!

Snap! That was Geoffrey's pencil-point breaking! Bother! Now he wouldn't be able to draw. He suddenly looked at Paddy-Paws and smiled.

"Paddy! Come here! I want you to take another note!" he said. He managed to write another note with his pencil and tied the piece of paper on to the kitten's neck again, and pushed her off the bed.

443

"Go to Mummy," he said. "Good little kitten, go to Mummy."

Again Paddy-Paws sped downstairs and ran to find Mother. Mother read the note quickly.

My pencil is broken. Please can I have my pencil-sharpener?

Mother stroked the kitten, and gave her a bit of fish for a reward. "Clever little kitten! Now you take this pencil-sharpener back to Geoffrey!"

She tied the little sharpener round Paddy's neck. "Go to Geoff," she said. "You go and find Geoff!"

And away went the kitten, up the stairs and into the bedroom! She jumped up on the bed and Geoffrey found the pencil-sharpener tied round her neck. He fondled the kitten and praised her for her cleverness.

"Cleverest kitten in the world! Very, very cleverest! Have a bit of my biscuit!" Well, Paddy-Paws thought this was a lovely kind of game – trotting up and down with something round her neck and getting a titbit each time!

444

Long before Geoffrey was up and about again she was the best little messenger you could imagine. Geoffrey was very proud of her indeed.

Now, some time after this, when Geoffrey had quite forgotten all about being in bed with a cold, the boy next door caught Paddy-Paws and wouldn't let her go. She wriggled and mewed, but he held her tight.

"I'm going to teach you how to swim!" he said, and took her to the pond in his garden. Paddy-Paws didn't like water at all. She mewed loudly and Geoffrey heard her. He was up on the wall in a second.

"Hey! What are you doing to my kitten, Tom? You stop that! You'll drown her if you try to make her swim."

Splash! The kitten was in the water,

terribly frightened. Geoffrey leaped down from the wall. He ran straight at Tom and Tom went into the water too!

Geoffrey snatched up the kitten and fled to the wall. But before he could climb over it Tom was out of the pond and after him, full of rage and fury.

"I'll teach you to knock me into the pond! I'll fight you! I'll knock you down a dozen times! How dare you knock me into the pond! I'll throw your kitten in again, too!"

Geoffrey knew he wouldn't get over the wall in time, so he raced down Tom's garden, hoping to get out of the gate at the bottom. But Tom could run very fast indeed, and he overtook Geoffrey at once. The boy swerved and ran towards a little shed nearby. Tom was almost on him. Geoffrey ran into the shed and slammed the door.

"You open the door and see how hard I'll hit you!" he called to Tom. But Tom didn't open the door. He locked it! Geoffrey heard Tom's mocking laugh.

"You're a prisoner! And here you'll

stay till you come out and kneel down to me and beg my pardon! Then you'll get a box on your ears and the kitten will get its tail pulled too."

Geoffrey yelled back at once, "You can wait for a year and I won't do that. Let me out."

"Shan't!" cried Tom. "The window is too tiny for you to squeeze through and the door's locked. Stay there till night if you want to."

Geoffrey heard his footsteps going back up the path. He went to the door and shook it. It was well and truly locked. Blow! He looked at the tiny window. He opened it but he knew he would never, never be able to squeeze through that!

"Blow Tom! He's a beast!" thought Geoffrey, stroking the frightened, wet kitten. He got out a hanky and began to dry the little thing.

Then a sudden thought struck him. He had to go out with his mother that afternoon to see his grandmother, who was ill. They were to catch the half-past three train. What ever would she do if he wasn't there to go with her? She would think something dreadful had happened to him! Then she wouldn't catch the train – and Granny would worry about their not coming to see her.

"Blow Tom!" he said again. "I simply must get out of this shed! Hey, Tom! Tom! TOM!"

He rattled the door again and soon Tom came up. "Ready to kneel down and apologise and have your ears boxed?" said Tom from outside the door.

"Tom, don't be an ass. I'm catching a train with my mother this afternoon to go and see my grandmother, who is ill," said Geoffrey. "I must go!"

"Not unless you do what I say," said Tom. "Well, call again if you change your mind."

And off he went once more, whistling. Geoffrey felt so angry that he nearly broke the door down! But it was strong and he couldn't budge it an inch.

He sat down on a box, panting. Paddy-Paws looked at him with big kitten-eyes. She wished she could help.

And then Geoffrey gave a little whistle and smiled. "Paddy-Paws, you can get us out of this! Do you remember your trick of taking messages? Well, take one now!" He scribbled a note in a page of his notebook, tore it out, slipped a bit of string through one end and tied the note round the kitten's neck. Then he lifted her up to the window.

"Go to Mummy," he said. "Find Mummy for me. Hurry, little kitten!"

Paddy disappeared out of the window. She ran cautiously up the path, made for the wall and leaped on the top. She jumped down the other side and sped up to the house.

Geoffrey's mother was upstairs in her bedroom getting ready to go out. Downstairs in the sitting-room was Geoffrey's father. He had come home unexpectedly, thinking that he too, would like to go and see his mother. The kitten saw him and ran to him. She jumped up on his knee.

He saw the note tied round her neck, and took it off in surprise. He read it.

Mummy, Tom has locked me in the shed at the bottom of his garden. He put Paddy into the pond, that's why I went into his garden. I can't get out. Geoff.

451

"That boy!" said Geoffrey's father, angrily. He had no time for Tom – a rude, ill-mannered boy full of silly tricks. Putting a kitten into the pond – and then locking Geoffrey up for rescuing it. He wanted dealing with!

He went next door. Tom's father was there and the two men had a few words together. Geoffrey's father told him curtly that Tom had locked Geoffrey in his shed and he wanted him out quickly.

"Oh, it's just a joke, I expect," said Tom's father. "I'll come down the garden with you."

So down they went – and as they got near the shed they heard the two boys shouting at one another.

"Are you going to come out and kneel down to me and apologise and get your ears boxed? And I tell you I'm going to take that silly kitten and throw her over the wall!"

"You're a cowardly bully!" Geoffrey shouted back. "You might have drowned my kitten, putting her in the pond like that. I bet your father would

452

be angry if he knew the things you do!"

"Pooh! What do I care for Dad?" shouted back Tom. "I do as I like. He thinks I'm the cat's whiskers! I don't take any notice of my dad!"

Well! His father could hardly believe his ears! As for Geoffrey's father, he smiled grimly. Perhaps Tom's father would now see that his boy wasn't all he thought him to be!

The two men came up to the startled

Tom. He was about to make a hurried explanation when his own father cut him short.

"Let Geoffrey out. How dare you do a thing like this? And I've got plenty to say to you about putting kittens into ponds. My word, I never thought to hear what I've just heard you say about me! So you don't take any notice of your dad, you say? Well, my boy, you're going to take so much notice of me that it will be a full-time job for you!"

Tom unlocked the door, beginning to shake at the knees. His father was usually easy-going, but when he got into one of his tremendous rages, all kinds of unpleasant things happened. Geoffrey appeared from the shed.

"Where's the kitten?" asked Tom's father.

"She went out of the window," said Geoffrey. He turned to his own father. "Thanks, Dad, for coming to get me out," he said.

Without another word he and his father went back home. Tom was left with his own father, looking very scared indeed. His father took him by one ear. It hurt.

"Now just come along with me and hear what is going to happen to you," he said, grimly. "So you do as you like, do you? Well, that's all coming to an end now. Come into the house, Tom."

Geoffrey was glad he wasn't Tom that afternoon. He made a fuss of the kitten and gave her some creamy milk as a reward for taking the note. Then he

hurriedly put on clean clothes and went to catch the train with his mother.

"Goodbye, cleverest kitten!" he said to Paddy-Paws. "I don't somehow think we shall ever have to be careful of Tom again!"

Poor Tom! He's very careful how he behaves now – and dear me, how he respects his father! That's just as it should be, of course. But what puzzles Tom is this: how did Geoffrey's father know that Geoffrey was locked up in that shed? Nobody has ever told Tom the answer – and I'm certainly not going to!

Good old Paddy-Paws. She's a cat now, but she's still just as clever as ever she was. She will take a message for you any day!

The Rascally Goblin

Once upon a time there was a little boy called Jack. He was a wonderful gardener, and you should have seen his flowers and vegetables! His sweetpeas were simply marvellous, and as for his lettuces and beans, Mother said they were better than she could buy in any shop!

For his birthday his father gave him a set of garden tools. Jack was delighted!

"They are really good ones, Jack," said his father, "so you must take great care of them. They are not cheap little ones like those you had before. Remember that whenever you use your tools, you must clean them well before putting them away, and you must always hang them up properly in the shed, and not leave them out in the garden."

"Oh yes, Daddy, I'll easily remember that," said Jack. "I do like good tools, and I'll keep them just as bright and shining as you keep yours!"

He did. He cleaned them well each night, and hung them up neatly on pegs in the shed.

And then strange things began to happen. Jack simply couldn't understand it. One morning he went to get his spade and it wasn't hanging up by the handle on its nail – it was lying down, and was as dirty as could be!

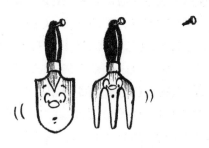

"Well, I am quite sure I cleaned it last night!" said Jack, puzzled. "But I must have forgotten to do it, I suppose!"

The next day when he went to get his watering-can it wasn't in the shed at all! Jack hunted for it, and at last found it out in the garden. How funny! He was sure he had put it into the shed when he had last used it.

Then there came a Saturday morning, and Father was at home to do some gardening too – and do you know, when he went with Jack to the shed to get his tools, he saw all Jack's new tools lying about anyhow in the shed, each of them dirty! He looked at them in surprise.

He was very cross with Jack. "Didn't you promise me that you would look after these beautiful new tools?" he said to Jack. "I am disappointed in you, Jack."

"But, Daddy, I did clean them and put them away," said Jack.

His father frowned. "Now, don't tell stories," he said. "It's bad enough to break a promise without telling untruths as well!"

459

Jack did not say any more. But he was very upset. He worked with his father all the morning, and when they stopped he was careful to clean his tools and hang them up nicely.

"That's right, Jack," said Father. "Now, listen – if I find those nice new tools lying about dirty again, I shall take them away, and you will have to use your old ones instead!"

Poor Jack! He knew that he always did put his tools away properly. He couldn't think how it was that they became dirty.

But the tools knew! When they were safely in the shed at night they talked to one another.

"It's a shame that Jack is blamed for what that rascally goblin does!" said the watering-can.

"Yes," said the spade, swinging to and fro on its nail. "He comes along and borrows us at night for his gardening, and never thinks of cleaning us or hanging us up properly."

"He's a horrid, nasty fellow," said the little fork. "He bent me the other day."

"And he loaded me so full that I thought my wheel would break!" said the barrow.

"I say! Won't it be horrid if Jack's father does take us away from him, and makes him use his old tools instead," said the trowel. "We shall be stuck away somewhere then, and never see the sunshine! Besides, I do like being used by Jack. He does make his garden so fine with us!"

"I've got an idea!" the wheel-barrow said thoughtfully. "Listen! I guess that rascally goblin will come along tonight. Well – let's be ready for him, shall we?"

"Ready for him? What do you mean?" asked the spade.

"Well – let's go for him and give him such a fright that he won't ever come here again!" said the barrow.

"Oooh, yes!" said the trowel. "That would be fine. I don't mind banging him on the head!"

"And I'd love to soak him with water!" said the watering-can, tilting itself up in glee.

"And I could run at him and run my wheel over his toes!" said the barrow, giving a great gurgle of laughter.

So it was all arranged. The tools got a come-alive spell from the little fairy they knew and they came alive for one night! The watering-can popped outside on spindly legs and filled itself at the tap! The spade hopped to the garden beds and filled itself full of earth. The barrow filled itself full of potatoes from a sack in the shed. The fork and the trowel practised jumping down from their nails, so that they might be ready when the great moment came!

462

Even the hosepipe joined in and said it would pretend to be a big snake! Oh dear! What fun they were going to have!

"Shh! Shh! Here comes the rascally goblin!" said the barrow suddenly. The shed-door opened and an ugly little head, with big pointed ears, looked in. Then the goblin ran inside and looked round for the tools.

"Where are you, spade? Where are you, barrow?" he said. "I've got a lot of digging to do tonight and a lot of watering too!"

"Here I am!" said the spade, and jumping up from the floor, where it had been lying ready with its spadeful of earth, it shot the earth all over the surprised goblin!

"Oooh! What's that?" said the goblin, alarmed.

The trowel jumped off its nail and hit him on the head, and the fork jumped too, and pricked him on the leg. The goblin scrambled up and ran for the door.

But the hosepipe was there, wriggling about like a big green snake!

"Oooh! Ow! Snakes!" yelled the frightened goblin. "Get away, snakes!"

But the hosepipe was thoroughly enjoying itself. It wriggled along after the goblin, and wound itself round his leg. The barrow laughed so much that it could hardly stand! Then it suddenly ran at the goblin, wheeled itself over his toe, and emptied all the potatoes over him. *Plop, thud, bang, crash!* How astonished that goblin was! He sat among the potatoes and yelled for help – but there was no one to hear him.

Then along came the watering-can, and
lifted itself up into the air. *Pitter-patter,
pitter-patter!* The water poured all over
the goblin as the can watered him well!
He ran to a corner, but the can followed
him and soaked him wherever he went.

465

The hosepipe laughed so much that it forgot to be a snake by the door and the goblin tore out of the shed and made for home. He was wet and dirty and bruised and bumped.

"There were witches and snakes in that shed tonight," wept the goblin, when he was safe at home. "I'll never go there again, never, never, never!"

He never did, so Jack was not scolded any more for dirty tools. They were always clean and bright, hanging neatly in their places. But oh, how they laugh each night when they remember how they punished that rascally goblin! I do wish I'd been there to see it all, don't you?

The Page That
Blew Away

Old Dame Candy kept a fine little shop. It was a sweet-shop, and my goodness me, you should have seen the sweets she had in it!

It was no wonder the pixies and brownies pressed their noses against the window all day long, pointing to this and that.

"Oooh – butter-nut toffee," said one.

"And honey-balls," said another.

"And peppermint rock and raspberry drops and sugar-marbles!" said someone else. "How does Dame Candy think of all these lovely sweets?"

"She has a magic book," said Snoopy. "I've seen it."

"So have I," said Pry.

Both pixies nodded their heads. Yes – they had seen Dame Candy's book.

"Have you read it?" asked one of the brownies looking into the shop.

"Oh, no – we've only seen it from a distance," said Snoopy. "We live next door to Dame Candy, you know, and one day we put our heads out of the window and there she was, reading her magic sweet-book in the garden."

"We saw her making her sweets from the spells in her book," said Pry. "We did really."

"Piles of sugar-marbles, dozens of toffee-delights, hundreds of candy kisses," said Snoopy. "She just stirred something in a jug and muttered some magic words – then she tipped up the jug and out came lots of sweets. She poured them into a dish."

"And sold them in her shop next day," said Pry. "My, wouldn't I like to get hold of that book!"

They had never been able to do that because Dame Candy kept the book under the rug in her cat's basket. Her cat always slept there, night and day, and if she wasn't there, the dog got in

to keep the basket warm. So Snoopy
and Pry had never a chance to borrow
the book.

But one day something unexpected
happened. Pry saw Dame Candy sitting
out at her garden table with her jug,
dish and magic book. Aha! She was
going to make a new batch of
wonderful sweets. He called Snoopy.

"Look – she's making sweets again,
using the spells in her magic book,"
whispered Pry. "If only she would leave
her garden for a minute, we might be
able to slip over the wall and have a
look at the book."

"She'd turn us into toffee-balls if she saw us," said Snoopy. "And sell us too!"

"Yes – we won't do anything silly," said Pry, with a shiver.

They watched from the window. Dame Candy had already poured a heap of brown chocolates from her jug, and each chocolate had half a cherry on it. They did look nice.

And then one of the chocolates rolled off the table on to the grass. Dame Candy bent down to pick it up. At that very moment the wind blew hard – and a loose page in the magic book flew up into the air! It flew over the wall into Snoopy's garden, and settled down under a bush. Snoopy clutched Pry.

"Did you see?" he whispered. "A page flew out of the magic book – and it's in our garden!"

"Shh!" said Pry.

Dame Candy was coming to the wall. "Snoopy! Pry!" she called. "A page from my book has flown into your garden. Please get it for me."

"Come down and pretend to look

everywhere," said Snoopy to Pry. "When you get a chance, put the page into your pocket. Then we'll say we can't find it and ask her in to look if she likes."

"Good! We'll read the page and make sweets all for ourselves!" said Pry. Down into the garden they went. Dame Candy had gone back to her seat. Pry put his head over the wall.

"We're just going to look for your page, Dame Candy," he called. "We'll hand it to you as soon as we've got it."

"Very well," said Dame Candy. "Look hard."

It didn't take Pry long to stuff the page into his pocket. Then Snoopy called over the wall.

"So sorry, Dame Candy, but we can't find the page anywhere. Would you like to come over and look?"

"No, thank you. I'm busy," said Dame Candy. "But let me warn you, Snoopy and Pry – if you keep the page yourself, and try to make sweets, I shall know it. Oh, yes, I shall know it!"

"We shouldn't dream of doing such a thing," said Snoopy, with a grin at Pry. The two went indoors, chuckling.

"That was easy as winking," said Pry. "Now let's see what the page is about."

They shut the windows and drew the curtains. They didn't want anyone

peeping in! Then they looked at the page out of Dame Candy's magic book.

"It's about peppermint rock," said Pry, in delight. "Our favourite sweet – would you believe it! Peppermint rock!"

"We'll make heaps and heaps," said Snoopy, rubbing his hands together. "What does the spell say?"

"We have to have a jug and a dish," said Pry, reading the page. "Well, we know that already. And we have to wear something blue to do this spell. Oh – so that's why old Dame Candy always wears a blue shawl round her! Have we anything blue to wear, Snoopy?"

"Our new blue caps!" said Snoopy, and they went to put them on.

"It's a very easy spell!" said Pry. "Look, we have to pour milk into the jug, stir with a poppyolly feather, drop in a lighted match, and then say 'Tirry-lirry-roona-moona-accra-rilly-POM!' And that's all."

"It seems very easy indeed," said Snoopy. "Is that really all?"

"Well, look at the page yourself," said Pry. So Snoopy looked. Yes, that was all.

473

They fetched a jug and a dish. They poured milk into the jug. They got their poppyolly feather from the cupboard, and then they lit a match and dropped it into the jug. What a fizzle-fizzle, and what a strange green flame!

"Now for the magic word," said Pry, snatching up the page. "I'll say it – and you can pour out the peppermint rock, Snoopy. I hope our dish is big enough!"

He said the magic word loudly and clearly: "Tirry-lirry-roona-moona-accra-rilly-POM!"

And then Snoopy at once tipped up the jug and poured out the contents. He looked greedily for sticks and sticks of peppermint rock – but all that came out was a stream of fine yellow powder!

"Pooh – what's this? This isn't peppermint!" said Pry, disappointed. "It's just powder. Something's gone wrong."

"I'm going to sneeze," said Snoopy, suddenly, and he sneezed very loudly indeed. "Whooosh-oo!"

He sneezed all over the dish, and the yellow powder flew up into the air at

once. Pry felt a sneeze coming too. He threw back his head and sneezed violently. "Whoooosh-oo, whooosh-oo, whooosh-oo!"

Then Snoopy joined in again, and soon both pixies were sneezing without stopping. The yellow powder flew all over the place, and the more it flew, the more they sneezed.

"What's happening?" gasped Pry, at last. "Oh, Snoopy – can this yellow powder be pepper? Have we made pepper instead of peppermint? Whooosh-oo!"

"We must have, whoosh-oo!" said Snoopy. "The spell's gone wrong."

There was a rap at the door. The pixies looked at one another, startled. "Who's there?" called Pry.

"Dame Candy," said a voice. "I've come for the page of my magic book. I told you I should soon know if you had it. I just waited to hear you sneeze – and you did!"

"Whooosh-oo!" sneezed Snoopy and Pry together.

The door opened and in came Dame Candy. She saw the page on the table and took it. The pixies went on sneezing miserably.

"You only had half the peppermint spell," said Dame Candy. "You have to read the bit on the next page in my book to complete the spell – then you'd have got a jugful of peppermint rock instead of pepper. Serves you right!"

476

She went out with the page of her magic book. Pry ran to the door.

"Take the pepper, please take it," he cried. "Whoosh-oo!"

"No, you can keep it," said Dame Candy, with a laugh. "It's all over your kitchen by now – you won't get rid of it for days. That will teach you to take things that belong to someone else, Snoopy and Pry!"

It did – and it was a dreadful lesson to learn, because Snoopy and Pry didn't stop sneezing for nine days. And now, it's such a pity, they can't bear even to look at peppermint rock. That starts them sneezing again too! They'll be careful not to meddle with Dame Candy's spells again, won't they?

Series 1

Magical and mischievous tales from Fairyland and beyond....

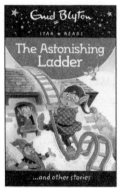

978-0-75372-644-0

978-0-75372-647-1

978-0-75372-646-4

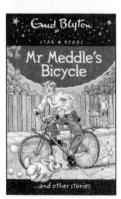

978-0-75372-645-7

978-0-75372-643-3

978-0-75372-648-8

Star Reads
Series 2

Enid Blyton

Magical and mischievous tales from Fairyland and beyond...

978-0-75372-653-2

978-0-75372-652-5

978-0-75372-642-6

978-0-75372-651-8

978-0-75372-650-1

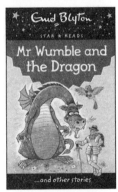

978-0-75372-649-5